PRAI

Lean, clean, and an exciting story! Love the twists and turns."

— *2018 ORANGE ROSE CONTEST JUDGE*

Jessie's Girl was a flat-out pleasure to read! Brilliantly written from start to finish. A story that brilliantly weaves together tension, conflict, love, warmth and a lot of WOW !

— TORONTO ROMANCE WRITERS *THE CATHERINE 2018*
JUDGE

I Rock !
2018 WINNER
NEORWA Cleveland
Rocks Romance Contest

JESSE'S GIRL

TARA SEPTEMBER

Hi Kelsey! ♡
Happy reading ☺
Tar ♡ September

DEDICATION

In loving memory of Evelyn Bonini, who encouraged me to write. I promised to dedicate my first book to her and I keep my promises, it just took 19 years to fulfill it. I'll love you forever Nanny.

1

hat the hell had she been thinking? Gwen Gallo-Clark hadn't been, obviously.

It would only have taken a few measly seconds to reach up on her tiptoes to look through the peephole before opening the oversized front door. Maybe then she would have been better prepared. Not that she could possibly have prepared herself for the sight of over a dozen reporters elbowing each other as they surged toward her. She wiped the sweat from her palms on her pants and prepared for the worst.

Thank goodness Maddie isn't home. Her daughter would have been terrified by the mob that confronted her at their door. Luckily, Gwen had just dropped her off at school.

She flinched from a particularly blinding flash of light from an expensive-looking camera with a lens so long you'd think the man was photographing Mars. Black and yellow spots appeared along the corners of her vision. Bringing her hand up she lowered her head to shield her eyes from the blaring lights. Being in the public eye was part of being a politician's wife—one of the things that Gwen detested. However, the press had never shown up at her home unscheduled or uninvited. And why were they looking for her husband, the Senator, here at his Texas residence and not at his offices or apartment in Washington, D.C.?

Pushing her anxiety aside, Gwen straightened and tried to look as composed as possible while standing there ill-equipped and barefoot, listening to the barrage of questions being thrown her way.

"Sorry, but one at a time please," she called out firmly to the crowd. "If you're looking to speak with my husband, he isn't here."

Her statement caused several of the journalists to laugh. One reporter quipped, "Yeah, we gathered as much, 'mom.'" Looking pointedly down at her chest, he aimed his camera and snapped a photo, which created even more snickering amongst the gathering.

Following the direction of his eyes, Gwen blushed at the reminder of what she wore. Black yoga pants paired with a loose gray T-shirt with scripted letters that read, "The World's Okayest Mom." She'd thought the self-deprecating shirt was rather funny, but not so much at the moment with microphones being shoved in her face.

Clenching her clammy fists, a sick feeling washed over her. Scanning the hostile group, she locked eyes with a friendly tabloid reporter she knew from her journalism school days and smiled. The woman's pitying look stopped her breath and for a moment, the spots in front of her eyes were back, nausea churning in her gut.

Those first terrifying moments of shock having passed, the reporters' words began to seep in.

"Mrs. Clark, would you care to comment on the allegations that Senator Clark has been having an affair with his intern?"

"Did you know about their embezzlement from the Literacy Foundation?"

"We have a source that estimates it is in the millions. Can you confirm the amount that's missing?"

"Have you heard from your husband?"

"Will you be stepping down from the Literacy Foundation?" The last question was practically spit at her by the formerly friendly journalist. Gwen mentally kicked her to the "can't be trusted" list.

Despite the disturbing accusations, her racing heart and sweaty palms, Gwen tried her best to mask her features to the crowd, wiping away all appearances of shock that she was sure were initially written on her face. No longer fully seeing the people in front of her. A bizarre sense of detachment joined the nausea. Not a pleasant feeling, but it was familiar. Once again, she'd lost control of her own life. Very much like she had shortly after marrying Congressman Jesse Clark seven years ago.

Tripping over her words, she managed to stammer out, "Nnn... No comment."

She forced the door closed then leaned her back against it, ignoring the banging and shouts on the other side. She slid to the floor and landed on her rear as if a carpet had been pulled out from under her—literally as well as metaphorically. *The irony.*

Staring out at the empty foyer, she said aloud, "Jesse, what the hell have you done now?" Once again, she had unwillingly been thrust into one of Jesse's schemes. Still, it was hard to imagine that his latest manipulations had meant to include accusations of affairs and illegal activities.

She had come to terms with the fact that their marriage was just another part of his career strategy, like a human chess game. She was simply one of his political maneuvers. Jesse had skillfully moved her from space to space until it was checkmate and all her pawns were gone. He'd won a game she hadn't even been aware they were playing.

It was only after the family man of the people had won his Senatorial seat, to much fanfare, that she'd discovered whom she had married. After she'd provided him with a child, published her article that catapulted him to fame, and was no longer needed to write his speeches, when the photographers were all gone, that was when Jesse's careful mask lifted. The side of him that no one else saw was exposed. A ruthless egomaniac.

Ever since, their "marriage" had essentially been over, except not in the legal sense and she'd eventually become numb to his cold-heartedness. But she'd never dreamed her career-conscious husband would do anything as scandalous as what the reporters were accusing him of. Not only to get caught having an affair, but to steal money? Jesse was always so meticulous and cautious about his public image. For him to give it all up in such an explosive fashion was incomprehensible.

Gwen sprung to her feet and went to the side table by the entryway to collect her purse. She dug through the ginormous bag for her cell phone, which had been set to silent and now showed seventeen missed calls from unknown numbers. But not a single voicemail or text from the man in question.

Logically, she should call Jesse to find out what the hell was happening. Yet she'd rather have called their mutual friend Reade Walker, to hear his deep and steady voice reassuring her. Regardless, Reade had left the country the week prior on a month-long work assignment. He'd be away for a few weeks and besides she didn't want to intrude. Instead she called Jesse's executive assistant while walking to her computer to do her own investigating.

∼

Reclining in his first-class seat aboard the double-decker

Boeing 787, Reade Walker glanced at the Barcelona skyline as the plane departed for Dallas Fort Worth International Airport.

He had been in Spain for a little more than a month, overseeing the legal entanglements of a corporate merger between a Texas liquor distributor and a family-held vineyard that produced one of Spain's acclaimed bottles of Cava. His client was eager to add the sparkling wine to their vast beverage portfolio, and Reade was called in to personally handle the contract negotiations.

The deal had gone smoothly enough, despite the translators involved and the necessary country approvals, but Reade had spent most of his time sequestered in a rented office space with an adjoining bedroom suite. The view from the plane's little window was the most he had seen of the historic city since arriving. Hell, he hadn't even tasted any of the Cava for which he had been preparing and negotiating contracts.

Although he would have liked to have spent at least one day sightseeing, Reade was eager to finally get back home.

The airline's flight attendant interrupted his thoughts about who in particular he wanted to see there, by offering Reade a selection of newspapers along with a none-too-subtle smile and wink of invitation. She was striking, with cat-like brown eyes, bronzed skin, and glossy black hair, but he wasn't in the mood to flirt. All he wanted to do was take a sleeping pill and try to rest for the duration of the eleven-hour flight. Taking a copy of the only American newspaper in the bunch, Reade barely let his eyes glance back up as he gave the woman a curt nod of thanks before unfolding the paper. Hopefully getting caught up on U.S. events would help him fall asleep.

The photo of an all too familiar face and the accompanying headline had the opposite effect. He jolted upright, but his seatbelt forced him down with a pained groan. Pulling the newspaper closer to make sure he wasn't seeing things, Reade reread the caption:

Jilted Wife of Alleged Corrupt Senator Denies Knowledge of Embezzlement.

By the time he finished reading the article—twice—Reade's blood was boiling. It didn't help that he had so many unanswered questions. The piece had omitted a lot of the earlier details of the saga which had apparently been unfolding for over three weeks while he had been incommunicado, sequestered in Barcelona. Worse yet, Reade had to wait until the plane reached the cruising altitude before he could get online and find out more.

Come on, let's fucking go already! They were still taxiing on the runway in line for takeoff. Reade felt like shouting in frustration, but that definitely wouldn't accomplish anything other than getting dragged from the plane by an air marshal. With no choice but to wait, Reade gripped his armrest and tried his best to relax. He was a patient man, after all. He could wait a paltry twenty minutes, right?

Drawing in a long, deep breath and then slowly releasing it, Reade let his mind drift. Like always, his thoughts turned to the "jilted wife" as he replayed their meet-cute in his head for the millionth time.

Even before he had laid eyes on Gwen at the local market all those years ago, he'd been thinking that the air was charged, almost palpable. He had scanned the quaint grocery store, which was older than most of the people in town, but he still hadn't been able to put his finger on what exactly was amiss. He'd felt almost euphoric and found himself smiling, and he hadn't even known why. Until that moment, he couldn't recall the last time he'd smiled following the grief of his mother's passing, the pain of which still clung to his soul.

Yet as he'd wandered the market on that fateful day seven years ago, he had felt his mother's love around him, guiding him as he'd gone about, randomly putting items into his squeaky shopping cart that was badly in need of some WD-40.

Turning the corner into the breakfast aisle, he'd been greeted with the sight of a shapely, denim-clad butt that was almost at his eye level. Not something he'd normally encountered while selecting cereal. The owner of said lovely tush had been boldly stepping on one of the wooden shelves, reaching for the last box of S'mores Pop-Tarts, just beyond her grasp.

Silently he chuckled at her determined pursuit of such a childish snack. He couldn't remember the last time he had a Pop-Tart. He was already intrigued, and he hadn't even spoken or seen all of her yet.

Reade let his eyes travel the length of the sexy stranger, from her backside to her long, lean legs, revealed all the more since her jean shorts were riding up, thanks to her extended reach.

When she'd continued to wiggle forward, stretching up on her tippy toes, he'd briefly contemplated lifting the unknown woman to help her grab the item—while also giving him a convenient excuse to touch her in the process, but he'd quickly disregarded that notion as wildly inappropriate. Images of the golden-haired goddess screaming and hitting him with her purse had given him pause.

No, the gentlemanly thing to do would have been to simply reach up and grab the box for her, but Reade had opted to take a different route. With a slow smile, he leaned his shoulder on the shelf alongside her, taking in the enchanting view a little longer.

Enjoying himself, he'd cleared his throat loudly and called out, with the tiniest hint of a drawl that for some reason seemed to charm the ladies, "Ma'am, please tell me if I can be of assistance?"

She started, like a child caught with her hand in the cookie jar. Swiveling her head away from the coveted pastry box, she looked directly at him, her bright-green eyes made larger with surprise.

That was it. Just like that, he'd been a goner.

Reade's breath had caught at her burgeoning, unreserved smile. He'd found himself reaching out to her even before she'd lost her footing and clutched frantically at air. A second later, the woman had conveniently slammed against his chest. Upon impact, he had foolishly thought that fate was his friend for allowing the object of his desire to fall right into his outstretched arms.

Relishing the feel of her, Reade had smiled down at her and said, "Nice of you to drop in."

He'd been pretty proud of himself for coming up with such a cool line, especially considering that his mind had stopped functioning the second their bodies had touched.

Thankfully, she hadn't screamed or pushed away, laughing at his quip and, seemingly, at her situation. She was petite and smelled like vanilla cupcakes. Reade should have released her immediately, but he hadn't wanted to. He would have kept on holding her awhile longer, too, if a firm hand hadn't come down on his shoulder, breaking the moment and bringing him back to his senses.

"Walker, get your hands off my girl," a smooth male voice had chided.

Reade had recognized that arrogant voice. Unceremoniously, Reade let go of "his girl." The pleasurable heat that he'd just felt run through him had turned to ice, as his long-ago friend—and current Senator—Jesse Clark introduced him to Gwen Gallo.

No, fate, lady luck, whatever you wanted to call it, had not been his friend that day. Of all the cruel tricks life could have played, having Gwen mixed up with Jesse had been a particularly low blow.

To Jesse Clark, everything was a competition, from petty

tennis matches that had left both Reade and him sore for days, to long nights spent trying to drink the other under the bar, to seeing who won the favor of whichever girl they had set their sights on. Sure, Reade had enjoyed taking Jesse down a peg or two when he could, but the difference was that Reade had never really cared if he'd won or not, nor did he begrudge Jesse his success and privileged background.

Or at least he hadn't...until that moment.

Until Gwen.

Just why losing Gwen, when he'd never even had her in the first place, hurt more than the parting of any of his real relationships, he couldn't have said. It just did. After all of his years being carefree and not wanting to settle down, he'd been brought to his knees. By Jesse's girl, no less. And no, the irony of that damn song was not lost on him. Although, he would definitely not recommend being around if it should ever play. A shattered radio alarm clock in a Chicago hotel could testify to that advice, if he hadn't thrown it across the room where it smashed into pieces. *If alarm clocks could testify*, he corrected with amusement.

Falling in love with a woman he couldn't have wasn't the only problem. The trouble was that Reade, try as he might, couldn't fall *out* of love with her. If it had simply been chemistry, his stupid, irrational feelings would have died down by now. Seven years later, though, and no such luck. It was hopeless, even stupid, but Reade was still wildly in love with Gwen and time had done nothing to change it. He'd probably inherited this fall-fast-and-forever trait from his mother, who had never stopped loving Reade's father, even long after the cold bastard had deserted them.

Ding! The overhead noise indicating that the captain had turned off the Fasten Seat Belt sign interrupted Reade's thoughts. Outside the window, there was nothing but clouds. After connecting his tablet to the WiFi, Reade quickly devoured every news story he could find related to the scandal, the knot in his stomach tightening with each piece. His girls' lives were being turned upside down, and he was still an ocean away.

Christ, you'd think they were my own wife and daughter. They weren't and never would be, but still his foolish heart disagreed. After all this time, Reade was used to battling himself on the matter.

Dismissing the unhelpful thought, Reade set his legal brain to work figuring out how he could at least protect Gwen and Maddie from the aftermath. He sent a message to his D.C. office requesting to schedule a call as soon as possible with their top political aide to discuss options. Until then, all he could do was sit and stew. If his will alone could have made the plane fly faster, it would have been landing by now.

2

*G*wen snapped her laptop shut after reading a particularly odious article about her life. *Jilted? Who even uses that term anymore?*

In truth, that was hardly the worst descriptor used to label her in the hundreds of articles published since the news of her husband's scandal broke. Clueless, naive, blind, foolish... Gwen had taunted herself with many of the same slurs over the last three weeks too.

With a frustrated sigh, she moved over to her bed and shoved another sensible sundress and sweater into her duffle bag. Unable to resist, she gave the mound of fabric a punch, wishing it was Jesse's arrogant face. The rest of her wardrobe was already set to be picked up that afternoon by the owner of a nearby consignment boutique. Truth be told, she was glad to get rid of the tailored outfits from her oppressive wardrobe as a Senator's wife.

Until recently, she had felt like an outsider in the small community of East Dodge. A tight-knit Texas town marinated in grit, heat, and tradition. It didn't help that she was the Yankee who had married their golden boy, whose family had helped create the town all the way back in the 1820s. To the townspeople, she had stolen their most important citizen. Only with the opening of the new library in town, which Gwen had personally established through her husband's foundation, had she started to feel like an accepted and valued member of the community.

Now, she was back to being a pariah, the interloper who apparently caused her husband to go crooked and cheat on her with his intern. Even those she had once called friends were now nowhere to be found.

The disaster that was now her life suddenly felt like a snowball that couldn't stop rolling downhill, growing larger with every rotation. The evidence of Jesse's deceit was almost too easy to follow. First, her husband had failed to show up for a vote, then it was reported his young female staffer, April, was also missing. This was followed by the discovery that the Clark Literacy Foundation's funds had been withdrawn to an anonymous offshore account, and finally, there was security camera footage of the presumed couple boarding a plane to Mexico, hand in hand.

Good riddance!

She wasn't sure which part of the scandal was the most mortifying: her seemingly charming politician husband turning out to be a scumbag and fleeing with his latest mistress, or learning about each betrayal at the same time as the world did.

What did one commentator write? Oh yes, "Fairy-tale romance is indeed a fairy tale." Ouch. But so true. It was hard to get too mad about that particular piece, since it so accurately hit the nail on the head.

The real shocker had come a week after the scandal hit, when the creditors starting calling. Apparently, her cheating asshat of a husband wasn't satisfied with only the Foundation's money. He'd sold off most of their combined assets without her knowledge, remortgaged his ancestral home that they resided in, and wiped their savings clean.

Surprise! You're essentially destitute, with your six-year-old daughter to support and no job or cushion to fall back on. Just an outdated résumé.

Unsure if she should laugh or cry, she'd done both since finding out the true depths of Jesse's betrayal. If she were being honest, Gwen had to admit she wasn't all that surprised by Jesse's callousness. She had long suspected that he had no real feelings for anyone but himself. As for her, she'd been whizzing through the seven stages of grief rather quickly since the news broke. But then again, she'd had the last seven years to prepare.

She wrongly assumed that Jesse's fierce ambitions would keep his more ruthless side in check. Especially since he had been determined to become the next Vice-Presidential pick, a stepping-stone to the Oval Office. For that reason alone, he had begged her to keep the image of their happy home alive. Since she had no interest in being a first lady, he'd shrewdly added, "If not for me, think of our daughter and the life she could have. You wouldn't take her father away from her, would you?" His guilt ploy had worked. She stayed.

Not that Jesse was ever around much, since he split his time between Washington, D.C., and East Dodge. Just enough to play up that good-ole-boy image everyone loved, especially if a camera was present. Whenever Jesse was home, or they had to attend a function together, they were civil to one another, and if Gwen was lonely, then so be it. She was willing to sacrifice her feelings, especially since they were responsible for getting her into this situation to begin with.

After all, she had been lonely back when she first met Jesse, who had been quickly making a name for himself as the bachelor Congressman in the House of Representatives. At twenty-four, things had finally been working out for her career-wise in New York City, having earned a coveted position at a popular magazine after she finished her master's degree. She'd never covered politics before and hadn't had much interest in it. However, her editor-in-chief said that her lifestyle voice would make for a more compelling and relatable account of young Congressman Clark, who was willing to provide their magazine with exclusive access to announce his run for State Senator of Texas.

It had been plain to see why there was so much buzz around Jesse. Although he was twelve years older than her, like everyone else, she'd been dazzled by his confidence and good looks. Still, she needed to know more about him than his sun-bleached hair and powerful charisma.

When he suggested they go out for drinks one evening, she leapt at the chance, hoping to catch Jesse being less guarded. In the end, it had been she who ended up being interviewed, and not the other way around. Jesse had been sympathetic while she told him about her parents' fatal car crash when she was a junior in college. With his intense stare and pointed questions, she had left that night feeling raw, like an open wound, and missing her family more than ever.

Before she could even think twice, he was holding her hand as they walked around his idyllic hometown in Texas, which he insisted she visit, followed by a dinner date that had nothing to do with business.

When her story had hit newsstands, it had propelled Jesse further into the limelight. Followed by an unexpected gossip column that broke the news about their budding relationship. They were soon being hailed as "politics' young darling couple."

Professionally, their relationship made her look biased and incompetent, and eventually she'd had to give up her dream position. He, on the other hand, had been delighted by the attention and commented on how one couldn't buy the kind of PR they were getting. He'd encouraged her to become his speechwriter and help him campaign for senator. A natural and smart career move, he'd informed her at the time. She'd never been excited about the idea, but Jesse had pushed and pushed until she gave in, the way she always did with him.

As if her fate had been a forgone conclusion, he'd announced their engagement in the newspapers before even proposing. But her initial reluctance became a moot point after discovering she was pregnant.

Now the downfall of her marriage was being covered just as enthusiastically by her former peers, not that she'd have expected anything different. *Live by the sword, die by the sword.* Unfortunately, she seemed to be the only one suffering by said sword. How she wished Jesse was the one being impaled by it. But no, he was getting off scot-free, having fun with a young girlfriend and millions of dollars. Probably lounging on a beach with tropical drinks in their hands, too.

Stop all the what ifs! It doesn't matter anymore. She was finally going to do what she should have done the moment it was clear that their marriage was just for show—get the hell out of Dodge. Literally. She would take her daughter and move back to New York, and try and revive her writing career.

Although just thinking about moving and probably never seeing Reade again had her feeling even more miserable, which she didn't think was possible considering her life lately, but it did. The same man she was now dreading calling and having to turn to for help.

No matter how much her pride protested, Gwen had no choice. The only possession of any value left in her name was the '66 Corvette Coupe that Jesse had given her when she had moved to East Dodge. Hopefully she could convince Reade to buy the classic sports car from her. She couldn't even afford the gas, never mind the cost of keeping a car in New York City. The parking alone cost more than rent in other cities.

As it always did, simply the idea of calling Reade caused her pulse to race in anticipation. It was foolish, sure. When would she ever learn? When it came to men, her judgement was obviously impaired.

Lesson learned. She would no longer leave her fate and happiness to a man. She needed to figure out who she was again. No more living in the shadow of Jesse, or any man.

Selecting Reade's name from her phone's contact list, Gwen held her breath as the line rang once before going straight to voicemail. Unprepared to leave a message so soon, she was caught off guard. Words stumbled from her mouth without time to properly think them through. "Hi, Reade... This is Gwen. How are you? I'm...uh, well, we haven't heard from you in a while. Maddie has been asking for you. I know you're probably busy, though, and I'm not sure if you're even back yet, but I have a proposition for you. So, if you can call me back or stop by soon, that would be great. Bye."

Ugh. Gwen groaned aloud. *A proposition? What the hell did that even mean?* Plus, she'd forgotten to mention the stupid car. No wonder she avoided broadcast journalism like the plague; she could barely leave a coherent phone message. *Oh, why didn't I script out what I was going to say before calling?* Hopefully she would hear back from him before they left town.

3

That SOB! That was all Reade kept thinking as he waited for his luggage to appear on the baggage carousel. He was cursing himself too, for not being around to help sooner. That at least he could remedy immediately.

Should he go straight from the airport to her place? Call her first?

When he turned his cell phone off airplane mode, several alerts and notifications pinged, filling his phone screen. His breath caught when he saw Gwen's name among them, indicating a missed call and voicemail.

He tightened his grip on the phone as her beautiful voice hitched, and she stumbled over her words. Things must be worse than he could have imagined for Gwen to call him with a "proposition." The term gave Reade a secret thrill, even if she hadn't meant it in an indecent proposal sort of way. Maybe she needed his legal advice? Someone to watch Maddie-girl?

Not wanting to talk awkwardly over the phone, with so much to say and so many questions running through his mind, Reade sent a text to Gwen instead.

Reade: Was out of the country. Just landed. Heard the
news. On my way!

Wild horses couldn't have stopped him from going to them.
It killed him that Gwen was suffering in public over the demise
of her marriage, still he was selfishly elated. Hopefully, now she
would see Jesse for who he really is: an egotistical asshole.
Hallelujah. Not that it would necessarily change Gwen's feelings
toward Reade, but simply knowing that she was out of Jesse's
hands was sweet enough for now. Almost.

Lost in his thoughts, Reade barely remembered getting
behind the wheel of his car or driving the sixty miles from the
airport to the lavish Clark mansion.

He leapt out of his car the second he shifted his Jeep Patriot
into park.

Gwen held open the heavy etched wood door before Reade
had reached the steps. His eyes hungrily drank her in as he
closed the distance between them, and he tried his best not to
flinch from the impact of her gut-punching smile.

He shoved his hands into his pockets to keep from reaching
for her. If only she wasn't so sexy in a plain top and snug jeans.
They hugged her curves in exactly the right places. Despite the
weariness in her face, she looked adorable. The simple olive-
green T-shirt matched the color of her eyes, but paled in
comparison. Her golden hair was pulled back in a smooth, high
ponytail, making her look even younger than her thirty-two
years. He loved seeing her dressed casually like this—a rare but
welcome contrast to the dolled-up, sophisticated Senator's wife.

Damn if Reade didn't want to tear her clothes off and comfort
her at the same time. The urge to do both had him stopping
abruptly in front of her. Any man who didn't want this woman
would be a damned fool. At the moment, he was sure he definitely
looked like one, standing there dazed and unsure what to say.

Before either of them could open their mouths to say hello, Maddie darted out from behind her mother. "Reade!" she yelled in glee, leaping into his outstretched arms. "Where have you been?" she asked accusingly when Reade set her back on her feet, but not before he gave her a bear hug.

"Sorry, Maddie-girl, I was working in Barcelona...in Spain," he clarified, allowing himself to be dragged along by his sleeve as the little heartbreaker tugged him inside. *Like mother, like daughter.* He would follow Maddie anywhere, too.

And although Reade still craved the effortless and almost instantaneous friendship that had developed between him and Gwen when she first moved to East Dodge, it was better all-around when he limited his interaction with her. But he wasn't able to hold back when it came to Maddie.

He'd been honored when Gwen asked him to be Maddie's godfather. A duty which he took very seriously, from helping to research pre-schools and thoroughly checking the installation of car seats when Maddie was little, to attending her big life events now that she was older. Last year, Reade had flown back early from a business trip to London, just so he wouldn't miss Maddie's kindergarten graduation, dragging his girlfriend at the time—Sheila—along with him.

Jesse, of course, had missed the celebration, like he had most of his daughter's recitals and any events that weren't scheduled by his communications team. Reade would never understand why Jesse wasn't as crazy about the girl as Reade was. And in Reade's case, he couldn't help but love Maddie, despite the fact that she was Jesse's.

"I know where Barcelona is," Maddie replied defensively, pulling Reade back to the present. Her irritation evaporated a second later, and curiosity took its place. "Did you see any mats or doors?"

"Huh? Oh, you mean matadors?" It had taken him a second

to decipher her pronunciation, but apparently he guessed right because she nodded eagerly.

"We learned at school that's what they call bullfighters there. The guys who wave a red cape in front of a mad cow with horns," the little imp recited proudly.

"No, I didn't. All work and no play for me on this trip. Anyway, I think I'd root for the bull," Reade admitted.

"Me, too!" Maddie laughed, and in another quick change of mood, she was suddenly frowning. "Did you hear about Father? There were a lot of cameras outside. My picture was in the newspaper, too. A photo of Mama taking me to school."

"Uh, yeah, kiddo." Reade glanced up at Gwen, who had followed them into the ornate living room filled with stuffy Queen Anne furniture, antiques, and gilded portraits of the Clark family ancestors. "I did, but must have missed that photo. I bet you looked pretty, though."

Nodding proudly, Maddie prattled on, "I had on my purple shirt with the glitter pony on it. It's my favorite. Oh, and I joined a softball league. You have to come see me play!"

Before Reade could respond to the little girl's rapidly switching train of thought, Gwen put her hands on her daughter's shoulders and pulled Maddie into a hug. "Honey," Gwen broke in softly, still holding Maddie in her arms. "I need to talk to Reade alone for a bit, okay? Big girl stuff."

"But he just got here!" Maddie whined, shooting her mom a disappointed glare.

"I promise, I'm not going anywhere," Reade soothed, bending down to her level and ruffling her long, sandy-blond hair.

"But we are," Maddie said with tears welling up in her expressive eyes that were so much like her mother's.

"What?" He brought himself back upright and turned to look at Gwen for confirmation, but she didn't meet his eyes. She ushered

Maddie out of the room, whispering something in her ear. "What did she mean by that?" he asked sharply when Gwen returned. *Were they going to Mexico to join Jesse? Was the intern just a ruse?*

"That's what I wanted to talk to you about," Gwen said, still not meeting his stare, "but not how I wanted to start off our conversation."

"I see," Reade stalled, deliberately taking on the calming tone he used with his clients to make them feel comfortable disclosing their issues. "How were you planning on starting?"

She gave him a grateful smile and a quiet laugh. "I was at least going to say hello first."

"Hello," he replied with his own small smile, yearning to give her a proper greeting.

Taking a deep breath, Gwen continued, "Then, avoiding the elephant in the room and without accepting any pity from you, I was going to somehow segue our conversation to see if you were interested in buying the Vette."

Of all the things he'd been expecting Gwen's proposition to be, it hadn't been that. "You want to sell me your car?" Reade asked, his mouth dropping open in disbelief.

"Yes, well, I'm currently low on cash and won't need it where we're going, so I need to get rid of it quickly. I know how much you always liked it. You used to work on it with Jesse..." Gwen let the end of her thought trail off.

Reade didn't give a damn about the car. He'd only fooled around with the stupid thing to be near Gwen, even if it was just to watch her typing up a press announcement for the campaign as she sat outside with her laptop. Absurdly enough, it was that same car that was now apparently bringing him near her again.

"I really hate to put you on the spot," she continued, "but I need the money to move."

"Move? Sorry, but we need to rewind a bit and talk about

the elephant. I don't understand why you would need cash. What's the urgency to sell the thing, or move for that matter?"

Sighing, Gwen sunk onto the floral couch. She patted the cushion beside her, inviting him to join her. Reade immediately walked over and sat next to her.

"Well, you might as well hear it from me," she said, then took a deep, fortifying breath. "Jesse took everything except the debt he left behind."

"Everything? What exactly does that mean?" Reade asked.

"He cashed out our savings and liquidated all our assets except Maddie's trust, but I assume that's only because he doesn't have access to it."

"That sonofabitch!" The chorus of every profane word he could think of started its repetition in Reade's head again. *How could Jesse have left his wife and child without any sort of security? How could he have left them at all? Another reason to hate the bastard.* Not that he had needed any more reasons.

As children, they'd been close, but when they'd reached high school, Jesse had suddenly turned on him, too. He'd told the entire school Reade's deepest secret, about not knowing who his father was. Lesson learned, though; Reade never confided in Jesse—or anyone—again. He could thank the jackass for that life lesson he supposed.

Then Jesse had showed more of his true nature, pursuing a brainy but shy girl from their class only to talk her into writing his papers for him and arranging for her to sit next to him during exams. Reade also knew Jesse had had something to do with their school's quarterback Hunter getting caught with weed in his locker, conveniently allowing Jesse to go from second string to starting lineup. Yes, Reade had learned the hard way that Jesse was unscrupulous and selfish, but deserting his family was a real dick move. Apparently he was no better than Jesse Clark, Senior.

Gwen sighed and muttered, "No argument there." She

slumped back on the couch, leaning slightly toward him in the process. "Apparently, even my wedding ring is a fake, a cubic zirconia. I tried to pawn it. The poor clerk thought I was a nut when I busted out laughing at that news. How appropriate, though, that even the symbol of our marriage wasn't real," she choked out, laughing and crying at the same time.

He eyed her warily, not sure what to make of her swing in moods. "But you still have the house. Why do you need to move?"

"The bank owns the house now, and it was never mine to begin with. Apparently, Jesse has been beyond delinquent in his mortgage payments, and I'm being forced to leave. That's why I want to use the money from the car to purchase two bus tickets and start over."

"But where are you going?" Reade asked desperately, still trying to process it all.

"A friend from college offered to let us stay with him in Manhattan, until I can find and afford an apartment for us."

Him? Hell no! To think, Reade had left the airport with a spark of hope. Woodenly, he asked, "You're going to raise Maddie in New York City, in an apartment?"

"Yes, what's wrong with that? I was raised in New York in an apartment," Gwen countered.

"I know, but not in the city, you were out in the suburbs. Besides, all Maddie knows is small town."

"Eventually, I hope to live in the suburbs again, but right now I'm just trying to make do. And at least in New York there are job opportunities for me."

Desperate, Reade pointed out, "You have no money, but you're going to move to one of the most expensive cities in the country?"

"That's the only choice open to me right now," Gwen answered sounding exasperated. "No one here will hire me, and practically all the big magazines and publishers are headquartered in Manhattan. I still have some friends and contacts there at least, and I'll start back at the bottom if I have to."

"You still have friends here, too," Reade replied, physically biting his tongue to keep from shouting: *me!* "What about your library? Your job here?"

"It's no longer *my* library," Gwen said, her voice hitching and her body practically sagging with defeat.

Only a few months ago, Reade had attended her library's grand opening gala. Gwen had looked stunning and regal in a gold sequined gown, quite literally resembling a trophy on Jesse's arm. The sparkling dress had only magnified Gwen's inner glow and the highlights in her wavy, shoulder-length, honey-blonde tresses. Reade had been so proud of her—his sexy librarian, as he often liked to imagine her. Even though Jesse had gotten most of the credit for the project in the papers, Gwen had done it all. The whole concept had been hers, down to the interactive music area and the computer lab. Jesse was the figurehead of the Literacy Foundation, but Gwen was its heart.

"What do you mean?" Reade asked, not able to resist gently lifting her chin and tilting it toward him so that she was forced to look at him instead of the floor.

Quietly she admitted, "I am no longer affiliated with the library or the Foundation. The library board made it crystal clear that it would be best if I stepped down immediately, citing that they couldn't afford a scandal so early in the organization's infancy."

"Those bastards," he growled, letting go of her chin with his heated reply. "There wouldn't be a library or a Literacy Foundation to throw you out of if it weren't for you in the first place."

She shrugged. "That was then, this is now. Easy come, easy go."

"But you did nothing wrong. Even the authorities have said that they don't consider you an accomplice," Reade objected, unable to stand seeing her so accepting of her plight, so nonchalant. He was raging over it himself. Almost every aspect of her life was now upside down, and she was ready to leave it all behind.

No way. He wouldn't let her walk away, not now, not after all this time. *And what about Maddie?* He couldn't imagine his life without her in it either. "Wait," he said, suddenly breaking out of his own selfish concerns. "You can't take Maddie out of school now, with only a little over a month left in the school year."

"I know, I wanted to avoid that, but really we have no place to call home anymore. I have no choice, we have to leave," Gwen said resolutely.

His heart lurched at the finality of her words. Yes, Lady Luck had, once again, deserted him. So, it seemed, had caution, for the moment. "Stay with me," Reade practically shouted, finally releasing the three words he wished he'd had the nerve to say years ago.

Eyes wide, Gwen took a second to respond. "Thank you for offering, Reade, but we couldn't put you out—"

Cutting off her protest, he insisted, "No, I mean it. Just 'til the end of the school year. The last time I checked, New York isn't going anywhere."

"That's really sweet of you, but I can't take advantage of you like that," Gwen said, shaking her head. "You're a bigshot lawyer. You don't need a social outcast and her daughter cramping your style. We'd drive you crazy, taking over your personal space like that."

You've been driving me crazy since the moment I met you.

"Like I care about any of that," Reade urged. "Anyway, Maddie isn't just your daughter, either, she's my goddaughter. I'm technically the next in line to take care of her, aren't I?" Not bothering to let Gwen respond, he surprised them both by reaching urgently for her hands. "I'm going to be in California this week anyway, so you'll have my place to yourself. It will just be for a few weeks. I swear it's not a big deal." Noticing her softening stance, he pressed further. "Come on, for Maddie's sake, let me do this for you guys. She must be really confused right now. Don't make her switch schools on top of it."

"You're right, it would be awful for her," Gwen agreed with a sigh. "But...are you really sure you don't mind? We aren't your problem."

She'd been his "problem" since the moment she fell into his arms. "I'm positive," Reade assured, squeezing her hands.

Relief flooded her eyes. "Oh, thank you so much, Reade," Gwen said with a big grateful smile that made his heart lurch. Letting go of his hands, she flung her arms around his neck for a quick hug. "You are a lifesaver. I promise you won't even know we're there."

I seriously doubt that. He returned her squeeze, his senses were already reeling from the chaste embrace.

He could almost still feel the warmth of Gwen's body, and smell her vanilla-scented lotion, as he drove home later.

What just happened? The resistance he had so carefully built up against her, brick by bitter brick, had fallen apart.

4

"I love sleepovers!" Maddie cheered from the back of Reade's SUV, tapping her feet on the back of the driver's seat along to the music. Neither adult commented on her innocent statement, but Gwen's thoughts strayed to her own sleeping arrangements.

She glanced over at Reade as he chauffeured them to his home and tried not to picture what his bedroom looked like. How accurately would it compare to her fantasies from over the years?

I'm actually going to be living with Reade. The thought repeated, but Gwen was still not quite able to process it. The idea was thrilling, even if it was just a temporary situation. It was the first good news she'd had in weeks, and she vowed to enjoy it while she could.

With a mental sigh of longing, Gwen looked at Reade as he drove. It wasn't that he was merely good looking, which he was, with rich, silky brown hair she dreamed of running her hands through. It was more the sensation of warmth and contentment that filled her when she simply looked at him. Those feelings were in direct contrast to the overwhelming sexual pull she also experienced around him, which left her far from content.

Stealing glances at his profile, Gwen reflected on the similarities and differences between Jesse and Reade. Both men were handsome and well over six feet tall, with powerful jaws and rugged features. Strength and sophistication radiated effortlessly from them, but where Jesse was fair skinned with blond hair and blue eyes, Reade was tan with dark-brown, almost black eyes and wavy brown hair. Both men were charming too, but Reade was more humble in that respect. Not coming from a legacy of money and influence, he didn't expect or take for granted the good fortune that came his way. Reade earned everything he had, whereas Jesse had inherited most things and contrived—or stolen—the rest.

They were both successful and beloved by the town, as well. Reade's prestigious firm had several outposts in cities around the world, and the only reason why such an illustrious firm had an office in East Dodge was because of him. He could write his ticket anywhere. Yet, he chose to stay here, employing dozens of members of the community. Gwen admired that, and so did everyone else. Still, he lived a private life. What would it be like invading his domain?

"I can't believe I've never even been to your place before," Gwen admitted, focusing once again on the road and not on Reade's alluring face.

"Of course you have," Reade replied matter-of-factly.

"I have?" she asked, puzzled.

"You've been to my offices plenty of times when we were working on the Foundation's contracts for building the library."

Of course I have. She had visited his offices other times, too. Back when Reade had still seemed happy to see her when she'd drop by to bring him lunch or to coax him into going for a brief walk for some fresh air, to get him away from his desk for a bit. That was years ago, before Reade had become distant towards her, back when they still used to talk about everything and anything.

"Sure, I've been to your offices, but not to your home," she protested. How could he not realize that?

"Gwen, I live on the top floor of my office building."

"Oh," she murmured, feeling stupid for not knowing that. She knew so little about him and yet feel such a powerful pull toward him.

"But your colleagues... Won't they see us and wonder what we're doing there? I don't want to cause trouble or gossip for you," Gwen worried.

"That again?" Reade huffed. "First of all, it doesn't matter what they think, I'm the boss. Secondly, there is a separate entrance to my floor. Thirdly, I don't think anyone there even knows that I live upstairs. They just see that I'm the first to arrive each day and the last to leave."

"Fourthly," she teased, "don't say I didn't warn you."

She didn't have to warn him. Warning bells had been going off in Reade's head all night as he told himself this was not a good idea, but he refused to consider the alternative. *It's too late, anyway.* Reade parked behind the historic low-rise three-story building, which had once been the town's bank. The first floor exterior was faced in gray cobblestone, with the top two floors built of a fancy red brick interspersed with lots of oversized double-paned windows that overlooked a small park across the street.

Despite the small town feel, he'd successfully convinced the other partners in his law firm that there was a lot of old money in the county needing trusts and wills, and wealthy family businesses in want of legal counsel and protecting. While all of that was true, mostly, he had wanted to open a branch here to be near his ailing mother and stayed after because of Gwen and Maddie.

As soon as Reade led them through the entrance of his penthouse, Maddie scurried around the loft's main living area, poking her head into cabinets and doorways, picking up knickknacks, and pointing out a picture frame that held her school photo. Gwen tried to call the tornado of a girl back, throwing Reade an apologetic look, but he shook his head and smiled. "Don't worry about it. Let her explore," he encouraged.

Maddie's enthusiasm was amusing, but he watched Gwen instead, as she glanced about his home for the first time. She smiled while looking around the open floorplan and Reade tried to see his place as she might. Lots of black furniture and empty walls, along with some mismatched items that he'd kept from his childhood home. The original, but restored, hardwood floors rolled unevenly under their feet. A black-and-white print of Venice from one of his travels abroad hung lopsidedly on the exposed brick wall, and a colorful woolen blanket that his grandmother had crocheted lay folded on the back of a worn, oversized recliner.

Reade had never expected to be living here for as long as he had, and he traveled so often that it sometimes felt like he used the apartment merely as a place to sleep and shower when not in the office. Now, though, he wished he'd paid it a little more attention. He tried not to cringe when he spotted the pinball machine in the corner. If that didn't scream *immature bachelor*, he wasn't sure what did. At least he had remembered to hide the framed photo of Gwen that had sat next to Maddie's before he'd left this morning.

"It's cozy," Gwen said, giving him a bright smile.

"It is?" he asked.

Gwen nodded. "I love the arched floor-to-ceiling windows. They let in so much light... And just look at all the decorative details in the crown molding. And the copper tile ceiling is exquisite."

Funny, besides the big windows, he had never even noticed the other details. Compared to the formal and vast Clark mansion, this bright, open room with lived-in furniture probably would seem cozy.

Spotting the arcade game in the back corner, Gwen asked excitedly, "Is that an actual pinball machine? That is so cool. I used to love playing them. I'll have to show Maddie how."

"I'd be happy to teach her. I don't mean to brag, but I'm sort of a pinball wizard," he boasted with a silly waggle of his eyebrows.

"Hmm, how unexpected," she said, giving him an unnerving, soul-searching look. "What other hidden talents do you have?"

He could think of a few he wanted to show her. The possibilities that ran through his mind, combined with actually having Gwen in his home, had his cock standing at attention. His current fantasy had him pinning her against the brick wall behind her, entwining their fingers, and fucking her until he was completely sated. Although it was highly doubtful one time would be enough to satisfy the lust he felt for Gwen. God, he was so hot for her he couldn't think straight.

A sudden loud vibration from her cell phone jolted them both out of the increasingly intimate moment. Gwen fumbled around in her purse, discarding a naked Barbie and a box of crayons in the process. She briefly checked the caller ID, then immediately hit the ignore button with a disgruntled snort. "Sorry about that," she said. "An unknown number, so probably a creditor or a reporter. Either way, I am not answering."

"The press is still hassling you?" he asked, concerned. "If they're calling your cell phone, I can help you file a cease-and-desist order on the grounds of harassment."

"There's no need, they stopped camping outside our front door before we came here. After they got the photos of the sad family that the crooked politician left behind, they went packing too." Gwen let out an annoyed sigh. "It's just that several television news producers have been offering me outrageous sums to do an exclusive interview on their talk shows. I'd be lying if I said the money wasn't super tempting right now, but I just don't want my words twisted anymore. I'm looking forward to disappearing from the public eye once and for all. Hopefully, the only time I see my name in print again it will be in the byline and not in the piece itself."

Reade nodded, noticing how tense Gwen had become. Until that moment, he had not fully realized how awful being in the public eye had been for her, especially since she had borne it so well.

"Why not write your own story for a change?" Reade suggested.

Gwen stilled, slowly looking at him in apparent wonder. Had he said something wrong? Maybe he shouldn't have suggested it in the first place.

"I hadn't considered that. I've become so used to being on the other side of an interview lately that I—" She stopped and gave a shrug as a smile started to bloom across her face, transforming her features from merely pretty to startlingly lovely.

Seeing Gwen's radiant smile aimed at him almost stopped Reade's heart. He momentarily had to catch his breath. Encouraged, Reade continued with his idea. "I'm sure a publication would eagerly pay for your exclusive story, and this way you would be in control for a change. There would be no middle person twisting your words, since it would be up to you what to say and, more importantly, what not to share."

"Do a profile on myself?" Gwen pondered aloud, her green eyes wide with surprise. "It's brilliant! You keep coming to my rescue. This is just the project that I need right now, and what better way to get back into writing again?"

He nodded. "By the time you're done, I bet you'll have the whole country sympathizing with you. After all, you wrote Jesse's most memorable campaign soundbites. You have a gift for making even the most mundane policies sound down-to-earth and relatable."

Was she actually blushing? Damn, she was sweet. And obviously in need of more praise if such a minute observation had her face heating. If she only knew half of how he felt for her, how much he admired her grace and quiet strength... Hell, he could drown her in compliments.

"Thank you for the vote of confidence, but that was years ago, and it's been so long since I've written anything and... I just feel like such a failure."

Reade stepped closer and locked eyes with her. Hers were slightly glossy from unshed tears. "Hey, now. Don't be like that. Failure is when character is revealed, and you've done nothing but rise to the challenge. Hell, I'm amazed with how well you're handling everything."

"Thanks to your help."

He shook his head. "No, you already had a plan in place, I'm just facilitating it along."

Shrugging, she slowly unfurled a small, vulnerable smile that tugged at his heart. "Well, I'm truly grateful. At least now, if I can find the right outlet to tell my story, I can go back to New York with a published piece instead of just a stale resume and a scandal following me."

Gwen's praise, combined with seeing her transform from the worried victim to the carefree girl that he once knew, made Reade feel like he had been handed the Nobel Peace Prize. Unfortunately, the mention of her leaving for New York again deflated his initial happiness. *At least my firm has offices in New York.*

"Uh, in the meantime, let me show you around," Reade

said, turning the topic away from Gwen going anywhere except on a tour of his apartment...and bedrooms.

Gwen in my bedroom. Suddenly, all he could picture was Gwen, naked on his bed, beckoning him forward. The image made his mouth go dry and shift uncomfortably. *Pull yourself together,* he chided. With great effort he tore his gaze from her and did his best to push his single-minded thoughts away once more. Instead, he turned toward the kitchen first, putting his back to the hallway leading to his bedroom.

The open kitchen, filled with shiny stainless-steel appliances, took up the left-hand corner of the main room and immediately drew the eye upon entering the apartment. Without any dividing walls to close in the modernized kitchenette, the space seamlessly flowed toward the wide-area living room, with only a round retro dining table and four dining chairs to separate the two spaces.

Gwen followed alongside him, almost bumping into Reade's back when he stopped to point down the hallway. "My bedroom is on the left there, and it has a connected bath. At the end of the hall is another bathroom. And the room to the right is the den, which also functions as my home office and pseudo workout room, but there is a sofa bed in there too. I was thinking—"

"That's perfect, Maddie and I can sleep in your den together," Gwen interrupted, before he could continue.

"I was going to say that you two can have my bedroom and bathroom, and I'll sleep in the den or out on the couch," Reade corrected.

"No," she protested. "We are already taking over your home. I will not kick you out of your bed."

Then join me in it. Great, now he had to fight the images of both of them entangled together in his bed that came flashing though his mind once again. Aloud, he said, "Gwen, I told you, I'm not even going to be here for the next few days, so you might as well take my bed. Besides, the sofa bed in the den is barely big enough for one person. The couch here in the living room also pulls out, so technically, we could all have our own place to sleep if needed."

She still looked unsure, and the way she was sucking on her delectable bottom lip had him biting his own tongue to keep from groaning.

"Please make yourselves at home," he said. "*Mi casa es su casa.*"

If only that were really the case, Reade thought as he gathered his garment bag and briefcase for his business trip, leaving his two girls behind. In his home. It felt disturbingly odd and right at the same time.

The big question was how he was going to manage to appear unaffected by Gwen or keep his hands to himself for several weeks—and nights—together in the same home. Good thing he was going to be away for a bit. He needed the distance so he could come up with a plan.

5

*S*he was having that dream again. She was lying in Reade's strong arms, and it felt so right having his body pressed down upon hers, imprinting himself on her. Gwen could smell his sandalwood scented soap and hear his thundering heartbeat as if it were her own. The dream seemed so real, she buried her head deeper into the crook of his warm neck, rubbing her lips there at the base of his throat.

Gwen moaned, wrapping her arms tighter around Reade, not wanting to be taken away from this delicious fantasy. She sighed with pleasure as his mouth blazed a trail down the column of her throat, nipping and nibbling and sending chills down her spine. Instinctually, her hips lifted up to meet his. *Wow! This dream is getting good.* She could even feel his...

Gwen's eyes popped wide open. She was, indeed, underneath Reade...in his bed. *When did he get here?* Her arms were wrapped around his bare back, stroking him. Her mouth had been pressed against the base of his neck. She could still see the moisture from her lips and feel the heat of his skin still on hers.

Holy crap. Tilting her head back, she peeked a nervous look up at him.

He was having that dream again. Reade squeezed his eyes shut, resisting the claws of consciousness trying to take him away from the glorious feeling of Gwen. He was winning the war, because Gwen felt so wonderful in his arms, kissing his neck, stroking his back. He let himself explore her fantastic body with his hungry mouth and hands. Needing more, he ground his hips against hers.

Oh yes! That feels amazing. His body practically hummed from the sheer pleasure of it. *A little too amazing.*

Belatedly opening his eyes, Reade rose up on his elbows and stared down at Gwen, who was wide-eyed and looking up at him in alarm.

Fuck. I was just dry humping Gwen. How did she get here? Reade quickly rolled off of her, and she sat up ramrod straight, clutching the sheets to her body.

"I'm sorry!" they blurted out at the same time.

"No, it's my fault," Gwen said, furiously shaking her head while avoiding eye contact. "I did not expect you back until later tonight, so I had Maddie sleep in the den alone, and I came in here to get a good night's rest. She likes to toss and turn and never stays still in her sleep." *Clearly, neither do I.*

"No, I'm sorry. I wrapped up my work earlier than expect-ed." *To get back to you,* Reade almost added. "The only flight available was the red-eye," he continued. "And since I'm terrible at sleeping on planes, I took a sleeping pill. I vaguely remember my driver dropping me off at home and then stumbling into bed. I forgot you were staying here. I swear, I didn't even know you were in the same bed until, well…"

They were both silent for a moment, hearts racing from the encounter. Finally, Gwen released a laugh that sounded forced.

"It's okay, we were both still sleeping after all, and it's not like we even knew who we were with. It was only natural." She got out of bed and immediately tugged down the loose jersey she was wearing.

Her attempt at modesty did nothing to cover her stunningly long legs, which Reade couldn't help but greedily take in. Man, did he want to devour her, inch by glorious inch.

As Gwen turned toward the door, Reade spotted his name lettered across the back of the shirt. *Is that my college baseball jersey?* Thoughts of Gwen as a college coed wearing *his* uniform flashed through Reade's mind, and he thanked the heavens he had the comforter pulled loosely around him to cover the evidence of his reaction. Gulping, he tried to call upon the heavens once more to prevent him from making a further fool of himself. Heaven must have been busy, though, since Gwen caught him staring at the jersey she was wearing.

Blushing, she shifted her gaze to his left shoulder.

"I hope you don't mind me wearing this. I sent most of my clothes to the consignment shop to sell and the rest is in boxes. I was so focused on packing for Maddie I didn't even think to pack pajamas for myself. This looked large enough, so I..."

Gwen glanced down at the floor. Her golden hair spilled forward in layers around her shoulders and face. *So, this is how Gwen looks in the morning after being kissed? Rumpled, flushed, and so inviting. God, her eyes are incredibly green.* So clear they reminded him of a piece of sea glass he'd once found on the beach in Key West. Reade groaned inwardly.

He wanted to pull her back down on top of him, wishing neither of them had woken up so soon. If only he had just a few minutes more, he would have lifted the jersey up over her head, revealing her smooth—

"Take it off," he announced gruffly.

Gwen's head snapped up at Reade's deep command. "Excuse me?" she squeaked.

Did I just say that out loud? He had been pleasantly thinking the words, but he hadn't meant to utter them. But he was still unable to tear his eyes away from her luscious body, taunting him underneath his jersey. Reade curled his fingers to stop from lifting the fabric to touch her.

Ordering himself to get a grip, Reade scrambled for a quick response. "Uh, I meant, take it! You can take it." *Phew.* He silently applauded himself for finally finding his brain. "Although, you can probably find some female clothes in the dresser over there that you're welcome to have," he said, pointing to a separate nightstand across the room.

"You have women's clothing?" Gwen teased, saucily putting her hands on her hips as laughter danced in her vivid eyes.

"Yes. I mean no," he said, rolling his eyes heavenward. "They aren't *my* clothes. They're Sheila's. You remember her? She left them here when we broke up. I actually offered to mail them and some of her other stuff back across the pond to her, but she said not to bother, and I haven't had a chance to get rid of them."

Oh, yes. Gwen remembered the regal Sheila, the English barrister Reade had met while working on an assignment at his firm's London office. Sheila had been smart and beautiful, with her porcelain skin and long, wavy black hair. She'd had a smattering of freckles on the bridge of her nose and crystal-blue eyes. Sheila belonged in a portrait, Gwen remembered thinking, immediately hating her for no real reason except she was dating Reade and looked like British royalty. When Gwen had heard they had broken up, she'd celebrated with a glass of wine, wondering what was wrong with her highness that Sheila had let someone wonderful like Reade go. Gwen should have felt bad for Reade after the breakup, as he did seem lonely.

And, really, Gwen hadn't wanted to see him hurt, but she wasn't sorry Sheila was out of the picture.

"Thank you, I'll take a look later. I have to go wake up Maddie, otherwise she'll be late for school." Gwen gathered up her things as Reade's hooded gaze followed her. "I found a job, by the way," she tossed back over her shoulder as she continued to the door. "So, I'll be able to pay you back for groceries and bills soon. Between that, selling the car, and hopefully some money from the consignment shop, I should have enough saved to head back to New York once school is out next month."

"Great," Reade said flatly. "What's the job?"

"Uh, it's in the food services industry," Gwen said with a quick slash of her hand through the air like she was literally trying to bat the idea away. She turned to snag her jacket off of the mounted coat hook behind his bedroom door. "It's nothing too exciting. I have the afternoon shift during the week, so I'll be home in time for Maddie. I'll only have to work every other Saturday night, but I'll be sure and find a babysitter for when I do."

Reade shrugged, obviously not concerned about the possibility she wouldn't find a babysitter. It was nice he never minded hanging out with Maddie. "Don't think you'll need the coat," he said glancing at his phone. "It's eighty-four degrees out, and it's barely eight o'clock."

"Um, just in case." Gwen blushed and clutched her jacket to her chest, rushing out and shutting the door behind her.

6

*G*wen looked so delicious, Reade couldn't stop staring at her. Plus, tonight she was wearing *his* robe, which was the beginning of another fantasy in itself. He couldn't take much more of this. He was only a man, after all, and this was pure torture.

It was like having half of a dream come true. Coming home and having dinner together like a real family. Reade could at least pretend for a bit. No harm, no foul in that.

Having half of a fantasy fulfilled was better than none at all, right? He would have given anything at one point to just have this.

Still, he wondered which was better for his sanity: dreaming about Gwen from a distance, or having her so achingly close, but out of his reach?

After dinner, Maddie went to watch television while Gwen gathered her plate from the home-cooked meal she had served. Reade's eyes and thoughts meanwhile strayed back to his robe and its current occupant.

The belt loosened slightly as Gwen walked toward the kitchen counter, and Reade's mouth went dry. The material was so long, she was practically tripping over the bottom of it, but boy if she didn't look cute and sexy just the same. He couldn't believe how much pleasure he was getting from seeing Gwen's body enveloped in his clothes. First his jersey and now his robe.

Reade ran a hand over his face, as if he could somehow rub away his lustful thoughts in the process.

Was she naked underneath? The images that now sifted through his mind caused a groan to escape from his throat. To stop himself from tugging on the flapping belt when she passed by him once again, Reade squeezed the glass in his hand so hard, he thought it might break. *Oh, dear God.* Being this close to Gwen was killing him.

Hearing his groan, Gwen glanced over her shoulder, raising one eyebrow in question. "I didn't give you food poisoning, did I?" she joked, but when he didn't respond, her teasing smile faded. "I know what you're thinking—"

He sure as hell hoped not, since his mind was pleasantly occupied imagining unwrapping that ridiculously big robe and backing her up against the counter.

"I used too much salt," Gwen said, sighing and shrugging her delicate shoulders. "Don't worry, though, at least you won't have to suffer through too many more of my meals. I should be out of your hair soon."

Simply thinking about her leaving had Reade's gut clenching, but he was still picturing her pinned between his body and the counter, now working her hands through his hair as his own fingers got lost in her golden strands. He didn't realize he was going to reply until he heard himself declaring gruffly, "That's my robe."

"You are awfully possessive of your clothes, aren't you?" Gwen started to laugh. "I didn't know what else to wear around the house, and I needed to get out of my terrible work uniform."

Still engrossed in his sexy fantasy, Reade barely heard

Gwen's explanation. "Are you naked under that robe?" he blurted out before he could censor the words. *Dammit.*

Gwen stilled, and then laughed. "Of course not," she said primly, pulling the robe tighter around herself. "I found a cotton nightgown in Sheila's drawers that I threw on. But I didn't think it would be appropriate to wear just that, which is why I pulled on this big thing over it."

Picturing the plain, long T-shirt dresses that Sheila used to sleep in actually helped calm Reade's jumbled mind and cool his libido. *No harm in those.* "Then just wear that. It's almost summer, and you look ridiculous." He sounded like a terse jerk, but he couldn't help it—he no longer had any blood left in his head now that it had traveled painfully south. Gwen looked unsure still, so he added, "Believe me, I can handle it if you can."

I cannot handle it, he thought a second later as Gwen shrugged out of his robe, murmuring something about how hot she was anyway. *She has that right!* He was definitely getting hot now, too. In fact, Reade briefly considered walking straight past her and opening the refrigerator door just to cool off. Somehow, Gwen had managed to turn an ordinary cotton dress—that made Sheila look drab and comfortable—into a centerfold shoot ensemble.

"That's better, thank you," she said, self-consciously looking up at him.

No, thank you. Reade would bet that he was gaping, but he could no longer feel his face to confirm. *Do men faint?* He could no longer pull oxygen into his lungs. He had to get a grip.

Heart thudding, Reade jolted up from his chair in disgust, cursing his own lack of control. He was behaving like a sex-starved maniac. Heck, he'd almost toppled over his chair in his haste to get away from Gwen. Or toward her, he wasn't completely sure. It was like he didn't have power over his own body or brain anymore; his actions were stilted, and his mind was in a lust-filled fog whenever he was around her.

"I know, it's tight and doesn't fit me, but you don't have to look so... so disgusted," she said in a quiet voice that sounded forlorn.

He had no words, so he continued to stare blankly at her. He was barely able to breathe at the moment, much less respond. *Maybe I really am going to faint.* As a precaution, Reade gripped the back of the chair that he had just vacated. Even more annoyed with himself now, he tried his hardest to recall what she'd just said and respond appropriately.

Reade replied automatically, with the only thought that seemed to come to mind, "Yes, Sheila is smaller."

There, he still could talk after all. He was silently patting himself on the back when he heard Gwen gasp loudly. He immediately spun around to face her, surprised to see anger flaring in her eyes as she slammed the mug she'd been holding down on the counter with a startling bang.

"Well, I'm sorry I'm not anorexic like her, but this is what a real woman looks like. I'd like to see how she looks after having a baby!" Gwen huffed and folded her arms around herself in what looked look like a protective gesture.

"What?" Reade asked, his voice husky. He resolutely kept his eyes on her flushed face, not letting them drift down to her delectable body. To be fair, he hadn't had dessert yet, and his body was dying for something sweet. A taste of her. *Really*, his delinquent conscience urged, *what's the harm in looking?*

"I don't care what your jaded mind thinks, I am not fat!" she protested.

"Huh? Who said you were fat?" Confused, Reade quickly glanced around the room in search of the nameless attacker.

"*You* just did!" Gwen responded indignantly.

He shook his head. "No, I didn't." For good measure he gave his head another shake in order to clear it. He was having a hard time following the conversation. *Fat? Where had she gotten an idea like that? And why is she mad at me?*

"Please," Gwen ground out. "You were staring at me open mouthed and horrified like I was the bearded lady at the freak show or something. Here I am, sweltering in your robe and already uncomfortable wearing some other woman's night-gown, and you rudely have to point out that she is smaller than me."

Reade burst into laughter, which judging by the annoyed look on Gwen's face was definitely not the right thing to do at this particular moment, but really he couldn't help himself—it was funny. He'd been worried she would see the lust in his gaze and the reaction his body was having simply by looking at her, but apparently she saw repulsion. He certainly hadn't meant to imply that she was fat. Heck, he barely remembered either of them talking since she'd removed the damned robe for his viewing pleasure.

He had to clear his throat before he could continue. "I couldn't help staring," he admitted after regaining his compo-sure, "but you've got it all wrong, I wasn't referring to your weight. I meant Sheila has smaller, um—" Reade managed to stop himself just before making hand gestures to describe the parts of her body he was talking about. He didn't dare look down at them again, either.

"Smaller...?" Gwen urged, looking at him like a wounded kitten, which made him feel like not only a sex fiend, but a heel to boot.

With no other way of getting out of this blundered miscom-munication, Reade finally blurted out, "Sheila had smaller breasts." *There. Done.*

"Well, I'm sorry about that, too," Gwen huffed, squaring her shoulders defiantly and raising her perfect breasts impossibly higher behind the thin cotton nightdress.

Reade cringed inwardly. He was staring again. It was as if

he'd never seen a woman's body before. But Reade knew the real problem. It wasn't just any body in front of him; it was Gwen's, and he had been dreaming about it for far too long to be unaffected.

Reade had learned years ago that not just any woman would do. He wanted this one. With anyone else, it felt like he was just going through the motions. He'd tried, dating others briefly, hoping they would help him to forget about Gwen, but it never felt right. The women had known it, too, which was why none of his relationships since meeting Gwen had lasted very long, and why he simply didn't bother trying anymore.

Reade's lustful haze evaporated when his eyes finally traveled back to Gwen's. She was more than annoyed with him. Pissed was more like it. He didn't know how to get out of this absurd conversation without sounding like a pervert, or, apparently, hurting her feelings. Since no response he could think of seemed safe, he gave none. Instead, Gwen continued speaking and he helplessly listened, unable to stop her erroneous tangent.

Gwen's voice grew louder. "I realize they add a few pounds, and I'm not one of the flat-chested, waif-like Kate Moss girls that you seem to like to date, but believe it or not, some men seem to like my boobs. At work—"

"I love your boobs!" Reade shouted before realizing what he was actually declaring in the first place. He wasn't entirely sure who gasped after that absurd announcement either—him or her. "Oh my God, why are we even talking about this? Time out," Reade said, holding up his hands in surrender. "Listen, I didn't mean it like that. You caught me off guard when you took off my robe. I was expecting a modest, loose night dress that I had seen a dozen times before, but on you... Hell, that simple nightgown makes you look like Jessica Rabbit! Believe me, I was thinking a lot of things just now, but definitely not that you are fat."

When Gwen's eyes widened with surprise or alarm, he wasn't sure, Reade quickly added, "Now, if you will excuse me, I have some work to finish." *Prying this foot out of my mouth,* he thought as he made his escape to his offices downstairs, determined to throw himself into his work and pretend that he hadn't just made an ass out of himself.

7

*T*he redundantly named softball team the East Dodge Dodgers were just about to start their third inning when Reade parked his car in the gravel lot and walked over to the home team's bleachers. A feeling of déjà vu crept over him as he looked around the same field where he used to play Little League. Not much had changed. Even the sponsors on the back wall remained the same.

He spotted Gwen sitting in the back row, away from the other parents and spectators, who kept looking her way before whispering to their companions. Gwen was definitely the talk of the town, and Reade could understand why she wanted to escape it. It wasn't as if the townspeople were mean spirited, they just weren't used to much intrigue in their small town. They couldn't help but be curious. After all, Jesse had put their town on the map, and Gwen was a local celebrity to them. It was gossip about either this or the new coat of paint the ice cream shop on Main Street had received. The scandal definitely won out.

As he climbed from row to row, Reade nodded at the folks he knew, but mainly he kept glancing up at Gwen. With this being a particular solemn anniversary for him, seeing her was like a balm to his aching heart. He eyed her long dirty-blond hair, nestled under a baseball cap, before moving down to her almond-shaped eyes and full, pouty lips. The last part caused him to lose his footing just as he lifted his leg for the final metal plank, landing him rather unceremoniously next to Gwen. Gasping, she reached for him in a flimsy attempt to help ease his fall.

Way to make an entrance, Walker. Then again, at least he was now cozied up against Gwen's side, her hand clinging to his arm. As he wiggled to right himself on the bench, Reade's arm brushed against her bare shoulder, shooting sparks through his already sensitized nerve endings. He clenched his hands at his sides as the urge to reach out to pull off her cap and touch more of her overcame him.

"Nice of you to drop in," Gwen said in a teasing voice, echoing one of the first lines he had ever uttered to her.

"Touché," Reade said, laughing. It warmed him to know she remembered. He sure as hell hadn't forgotten.

Clearing his throat, Reade looked out at the game to find Maddie fielding a ground ball at second base and tagging the runner for an out. He came to his feet, cheering and calling out her name. Apparently she heard his voice because Maddie turned from the base, beamed, and waved her glove at them. The joy on her face and unabashed reaction had Reade swelling with pride

"Sorry, I'm late. How are they doing?" Reade asked, turning to Gwen as he sat back down on the bench.

"You made it just in time. That play was definitely the high-light so far," Gwen said with a bright smile.

They fell into a comfortable silence, watching the game, clapping when appropriate, and waving to Maddie whenever she looked their way.

As the innings stretched on, the spring air turned unexpectedly cool. Attuned to Gwen as he was, Reade couldn't help but notice the chill that ran through her body when a sudden gust of wind hit them. He was in such a state of heightened awareness whenever he was around her, Reade felt every little movement Gwen made without having to look at her. It was his own personal hell. Reade shrugged off his navy sports coat and draped it around Gwen's shoulders, allowing his fingers to trail down her uncovered arms in the process.

This time, he couldn't be sure if her shudder was from his touch or the cold, but it took all his strength to resist wrapping his arms around her to offer additional warmth. Instead, he simply nodded as Gwen thanked him and eyed the dark cloud looming ominously in the distance. He was completely taken aback when Gwen rested her delicate hand on his leg.

"How are you doing today?" she asked, her tone turning serious.

"Um..." Reade muttered, completely at a loss for words. He could no longer remember how he felt about anything except for the slight pressure of her hand on his thigh.

"It's the anniversary of your mother's passing, right?" Gwen asked solemnly, looking tenderly into his eyes as if she could see into his soul. The gloomy weather was making him fanciful.

"Yes, but how did you know?" he whispered in amazement.

"That afternoon we visited her grave together, while Jesse was busy preparing for some public appearance. I remember the engraved date on the headstone."

"Of course," Reade said, thinking back to that fall day when she'd offered to accompany him. "You placed a little pumpkin on the ground in front of her plot. Come winter, it was the only bit of color on the ground, so I left it there. I guess it must have rotted into the soil before the grounds crew saw it, because by the following fall a pumpkin patch had grown there. It felt magical."

"Oh, I love that," Gwen said with watery eyes that made the green depths even greener.

"My mom would have loved it, too. Halloween was her favorite holiday," Reade said wistfully. He often wished the two women had really known each other, but he wished for a lot of things when it came to Gwen. "The grounds crew, on the other hand, did *not* love it. They called telling me to remove the impromptu patch, citing that it was a cemetery, not a garden, and that they didn't want an infestation of rodents and creatures to deal with."

"That's harsh. I'm sorry if I got you in trouble," Gwen said, patting his leg in comfort. Distracting that, Reade thought, trying to remember what he was about to say.

"Believe me, I was harsh back," Reade recalled with a smile. "I told them they better not touch one single pumpkin, pointing out that the bylaws and rules of the cemetery stated that no citrus plants or vegetables could be planted, but nothing regarding other fruits or gourds was listed. Then, I threw out some legalese that had them backing down and later amending the contracts for incoming gravesites to prohibit pumpkin patches."

Gwen let out a throaty little chuckle that sounded low and intimate. "It must be nice to be a lawyer, to have the power to get whatever you want."

"Not everything," Reade said firmly, once again focusing on her lips. He might have imagined it, but for a second it seemed she was starting to lean towards him. The roaring crowd coming to their feet around them had Gwen jumping back and removing her hand from his thigh. Clearing his throat, Reade tried to revive their conversation. "That's why I was late. I stopped by her grave before coming here."

"I thought you might," Gwen said, leaning close again. "I'm sure you think about her often, but anniversaries and birthdays tend to be especially difficult. At least it's that way for me. You know, I always valued our talks about our shared grief, especially since back then, there weren't many people our age who had experienced that kind of pain and loss."

"I know," Reade nodded. "They were important to me, too."

"Well, I'm still here if you ever need to talk," Gwen offered.

For now, Reade thought, automatically bobbing his head again in response. *But what about in a few more weeks when Maddie is out of school? What then?* It would be another loss Reade wasn't sure he could take.

When the rain started, his gloomy mood welcomed it. He cheered up some when Gwen protectively slung his jacket over their heads, bringing them into a huddle. Her arm stretched along his shoulders and hugged him close, in order to keep him covered from the heavy drops of rain that battered against the woolen material.

Frankly, Reade couldn't care less if he got soaked or not, but he was more than willing to hide out with Gwen in the intimate space that she had created just for them, blocking out everything except one another. The delighted, husky melody of her laughter made Reade instantly hard. He set his jaw against the familiar rush of lust, but her sweet vanilla scent teased his senses and had him wondering, not for the first time, if she tasted as good as she smelled.

The drumming feet of the people fleeing the bleachers caused the metal bench beneath them to vibrate, reminding Reade that they were, sadly, not alone.

"We better go before lightning strikes. Here, you take it, I have a hat on," Gwen said with a grin, shifting his coat entirely over to cover him. "Looks like the kids are safely in the dugout. Counting aloud to three, she took off toward her car with a seemingly delighted squeal.

Oh, for fuck's sake. Of course she's wearing a freaking white T-

shirt. Reade groaned as he sprinted behind Gwen to the parking lot, not sure if he should thank or curse the rain, after all. Regardless, the sight of her in the nearly transparent material that clung to her lush curves would forever be burned into Reade's brain.

8

---

*G*wen hummed to herself as she prepared dinner for Maddie. *And Reade*, she thought with a surge of happiness. The first time she'd cooked for him, Reade had seemed shocked and unsure as he'd entered his apartment and seen them in the kitchen, waiting for him to join. Gwen smiled remembering the surprise in his eyes. Reade had almost seemed embarrassed. He even protested, telling her that she didn't have to make anything for him, that he normally ordered in or heated something up.

Sure, Gwen knew that she was being fanciful, pretending that she was Reade's wife, but she truly enjoyed being able to cook for him. It made her happy, knowing she could, at least, take care of him in this regard.

Although she cooked regularly for Maddie, she hadn't laid out placemats for three in, well, it seemed like forever. Doing so now had her smiling and glancing at the door again, for the dozenth time. Excitement danced in her belly at the thought of Reade finally walking through that door. To her.

Okay, so really he was returning to his home and not to see her specifically, but what harm was there in pretending? Yes, she was going to miss this intimacy after she and Maddie left. But she was going to miss him either way, and now she would at least have some happier memories to draw upon. *God, he's delicious,* she thought with a familiar pang of longing.

Each day, it was getting harder not to tackle Reade and lay a thousand kisses on him when he entered the apartment. With a shake of her head, Gwen tried her best to ward off the crazy impulse. *This is ridiculous. He's not even home yet.* Her imagination was out of control, being in such close proximity to Reade each day. At least he was no longer frowning at her all the time. They were becoming friends again, or she hoped they were.

Was she just imagining the tenderness she sometimes glimpsed in Reade's mysterious, dark eyes, during those times when his gaze met hers? Since the incident a few nights ago— the unrobed revelation, as she liked to call it—Reade's behavior had stayed mostly the same. The attraction he claimed to have felt sadly seemed to have been a freak occurrence. Although, it didn't stop her from recalling the flash of male appreciation that had heated his gorgeous eyes. In a matter of seconds, she had gone from feeling like a frumpy mommy to hearing a rather flattering, albeit reluctant, confession.

Grow up, already. Didn't your first go-around with love teach you anything? This was real life. *Just because you like someone, doesn't mean they are going to like you back.* Being in close quarters wasn't going to change anything.

"Madilyn," Gwen called out, a little harsher than she had intended. Gentling her tone, she instructed, "Come finish setting the table, please."

Her daughter dutifully closed her school book and left it out on the coffee table in the living room, glancing behind her to the front door. They had fallen into a pleasant routine of Reade coming home for dinner together, and afterward he would review Maddie's homework. Gwen had normally done that herself, but Maddie, the little traitor, had declared that she only wanted Reade to do it. In fact, her exact words were, "Not you, Mommy."

Gwen could hardly blame her daughter for wanting to spend time with Reade. She wanted to do the same thing, but unfortunately she didn't have Maddie's excuse.

Jesse only used to ask about Maddie's grades, never once showing any real interest in what she was actually learning, and he definitely never helped with her homework. Beyond having a child for the sake of his public image, Jesse had had no interest in being a father of any kind, much less one who was involved in every aspect of his child's life. The kind of dad that Reade would be one day. Watching him and Maddie each night, their heads huddled together, their occasional laughter, was enough to make Gwen's whole body melt on the spot. It was maternal overload.

Gwen brought herself back from her daydreams to find Maddie was humming, too, as she placed forks and knives at each place setting. Gwen sighed. It was going to be a lot harder to leave now that Reade had become a bigger part of their lives. For both of them.

Reade took his usual seat at the dining table. Having Gwen and Maddie by his side, in his home, was a sweet torture. His senses were constantly on overload. From coming home and being greeted by Maddie propelling herself into his arms with enthusiastic abandon, to simply catching Gwen's fragrance lingering in the hallway. He liked it even better now that she smelled like a mix between his soap and something that was uniquely Gwen. It was agony. They were everywhere, and he was falling harder for both of them, which he hadn't thought possible.

It was just a matter of time before Gwen saw right through him, and then what? Would she leave sooner?

Just the thought of them leaving in two weeks had him in a foul mood. He couldn't very well stop them from going once school let out and they no longer had a reason to stay with him, but he couldn't prevent himself from hoping that maybe Gwen would change her mind. That something would change.

At the very least, Reade wanted to help them in the ways that he could, especially in regards to further harm from Jesse. Yes, Jesse Clark was out of their lives now, but the ambiguity of the situation did not sit well with the lawyer in Reade. Hell, they didn't even know where Jesse was at the moment, and that left Reade uneasy. Gwen and Maddie deserved closure.

Yup, closure would help Gwen to move on, especially in her career. Without having the corrupt Clark name connected to hers, Gwen could start over. And, just maybe, that would get Gwen thinking about moving on in other ways, too. It would also make Reade feel a lot better, knowing that, legally, Gwen was no longer Jesse's girl, even if she wasn't his, either.

"Um, Gwen?" Reade asked, once Maddie had left the dinner table to put on her pajamas. Before being excused, she'd made him promise to review her homework, which he always looked forward to. Reade cherished the quiet moments he spent with Maddie looking over her school work. Listening to her silly stories about her day had him falling deeper and deeper.

"Yes?" Gwen answered, looking at him rather intently from across the table.

Seeing her beautiful eyes focused on his caused Reade to clear his throat, in an effort to remember just what he had been about to say. "I know you've been dealing with a lot, just figuring out how to get by lately, but have you thought about getting a divorce?"

She hesitated for a second. "With Jesse gone so suddenly and completely, I feel like I already am divorced. But yes, I would like to make it official. Once we're settled into our new life and can afford it, I plan to contact a lawyer to discuss my options."

"You do realize you're sitting across from a lawyer now, right?" Reade teased.

Gwen exhaled a small huff. "Yes, but you're not a divorce lawyer," she pointed out with a saucy and tempting arch of her brow.

"No, but I am partner and part-owner of a law firm that employs lawyers with various areas of expertise. In fact, Danielle Dixon would be perfect for you. She's a great divorce attorney, and our best at family law. I trust her skill implicitly, and since I travel so much, she's often my right-hand woman overseeing the firm."

It was irrational, but Gwen couldn't help the pang of jealousy that seared through her. How she wished she could be described as Reade's right-hand woman. Or just his woman. It didn't help that Danielle Dixon, a tall, long-legged, chestnut-haired beauty, was also smart and genuinely kind. Picturing Reade working alongside Danielle made Gwen's throat constrict.

She had only met the woman once, at the library's opening gala. Danielle had attended with most of Reade's coworkers, all of whom had helped provide counsel for the project. Even then, Gwen had felt envious of Danielle when she had spotted Reade across the room talking to the lovely woman. Simply knowing that Reade preferred brunettes had caused Gwen to cross the room and interrupt them, before she could think twice. She'd soon felt contrite when Danielle greeted her warmly and praised Gwen for her work with the library and the important national role that the Foundation would serve. Then Danielle had professed that she was planning on volunteering in the new ESL program, an initiative Gwen had pushed for.

No, Gwen couldn't justify her resentment. In fact, Danielle seemed like someone Gwen would have been friends with if she could get over her unfounded jealousy. And Reade and Jesse had known Danielle since they were kids. Apparently, Jesse had taken Danielle to prom, but picturing the two of them together didn't tie Gwen's stomach in knots. It was the possibility of Danielle with Reade that made her ill with envy.

"I can have Dani make room in her schedule for you, if you'd like," Reade said, breaking Gwen from her disheartening thoughts. "Pro bono of course," he rushed to add, when she had still not responded.

"Really? Won't that raise some eyebrows with your partners?" She didn't feel great, accepting the favor, but it would be a relief to know she would be getting the ball rolling on dissolving her last tie with Jesse.

"I've never prevailed upon them for my own legal needs before, and the firm is at the disposal of all employees or their families if a situation should arise." Reade smiled and fiddled with his placemat. "Besides, my partners have all been divorced more than once, so they can hardly gripe at me dipping into billable hours."

Gwen wanted to argue that she wasn't family, but saying so would hurt. Maybe Reade being Maddie's godfather would count as being a family member, who knew? Gwen held her tongue, not wanting to look that proverbial gift horse in the mouth, especially since she was unable to see an affordable alternative. "Thank you, but I'm not sure when I can meet with her. I take Maddie to school in the mornings, work until late afternoon, and then need to be back here when school lets out. We have dinner, and then I'm up most of the night working on my story," Gwen pointed out.

"Don't worry, we'll figure it out," Reade said. Then, seeming to give it some thought, he added, "Actually, this Thursday I was hoping to leave work early to catch Maddie's softball game. I can take her and bring her back, while you meet with Danielle. If you think that will work, I can double check Dani's calendar in the morning and let you know for sure."

"That would be great, and I know Maddie would be so proud to have you attend her game again. I think she might have joined the team in the first place because she knows you used to play baseball," Gwen admitted.

Now, didn't that just tug at Reade's heart? The sudden lump in his throat kept him from eating the last bite of his meal. Instead, he pushed his plate away. Yup, he was definitely going to be in trouble when they left. *One problem at a time.* Just like a contract, figure out point A before worrying about point Z. He calmed at his own instructions, clinging to the slightest semblance of a plan.

"Did you know?" Gwen asked while turning on the faucet, dragging him out of his melancholy thoughts. So lost in his plan he hadn't even realized she had left the table.

"Know what?" Reade answered absentmindedly, picking up his plate from the dinette and bringing it over to the counter where she stood.

"That Jesse was having an affair?" she asked point blank.

"Hell, no. If I had known that, believe me, I would have done something." *Like do everything in my power to convince you and Maddie to run away with me instead of staying with that selfish asshole.* But no, Jesse knew better than to have indicated that there were any problems between him and Gwen. That would have been like handing Reade a gift, and Jesse would be the last person to do him a kindness.

Ever since that first gloating "my girl" comment in the grocery store, Jesse had always been sure to snidely make clear that he knew about Reade's feelings toward Gwen. Not that Reade would ever confirm it.

After the first year of marriage, Jesse and Gwen had no longer been hanging all over each other, and they seemed a bit distant. Reade had assumed that their relationship had grown more comfortable over the years.

Although from Jesse's telling of it, whenever he would return home, their love life was hotter than ever. Many times, Reade had bitten his own cheek, drawing blood as he listened to Jesse overshare about their sex life and how wild it was. Imagining Gwen's hot, curvaceous body was enough to make Reade storm out or chug his drink in frustration and longing. Anything to keep from punching Jesse for knowingly torturing him.

Bringing him out of his envious thoughts, Gwen said, "Jesse doesn't deserve to have a loyal friend like you."

Reade covered his self-deprecating laugh with a cough. That was the most absurd thing he had ever heard. A man who'd been lusting after the wife of his so-called friend for seven years could hardly be called a loyal anything. "He doesn't deserve a wife like you," Reade replied before he could think the better of it.

She beamed. "That was nice of you to say."

He shrugged, and they fell into a comfortable silence as they cleaned and dried the dishes together in a seamless rhythm, as if they had been doing the same domestic routine for years.

"Did *you* know?" Reade asked eventually. The question had been bugging him.

"Yes and no," Gwen said, dismissively, shrugging her slim shoulders. "I never knew for sure, but I assumed he must be seeing other women while he was hundreds of miles away. Especially, since we hadn't been intimate in years."

Reade jerked around to stare at her. Dumfounded, he nearly let the dish she had just handed him slip from his fingers.

"Years?" he croaked.

Gwen nodded. "Jesse said it would be wise to keep separate bedrooms after Maddie was born."

He couldn't believe it. "But that was over six years ago, and in all that time... You two...?" Reade trailed off, shaking his head in disbelief. *Impossible. It's been two weeks, and I can barely keep my hands off of her.*

Gwen eyed him as he coughed. She gave him several soft taps on the back. "Are you okay?" she asked, her hand now soothingly rubbing his shoulders. "I'm embarrassing you, aren't I? Sorry, I really shouldn't have shared that. He is your friend, after all, and that wasn't... Believe me, I don't usually go around advertising that part of our marriage."

Despite the subject matter, Reade was so relieved, he couldn't stop his lips from spreading into a dopey smile. "No. I'm glad you did." Okay, grinning like a fool probably seemed odd and possibly rude, but damn, he liked what he was hearing. It was like he could suddenly breathe easier than he had in years. In fact, he felt so ridiculously happy, he wanted to pull Gwen into his arms and lift her into the air in celebration.

Gwen tentatively smiled in return, but then her smile abruptly disappeared. He immediately wanted it back.

Rewashing an already clean glass, she looked everywhere but at him. "I know you don't like me much, Reade," she said, squaring her shoulders. "I'm not sure what I did to cause you to stop talking to me, but I do hope we are becoming friends again. Even without Jesse around, and not just for Maddie's sake either. You and me."

"You and me?" Reade repeated wistfully, enjoying hearing the pairing said out loud, before realizing what she'd said. "Who said I didn't like you?"

"Come on, Reade." Gwen rolled her eyes. "No one had to tell me."

"What do you mean?" He wasn't following.

"You were so nice to me in the beginning, but later you would hardly talk to me. And when you would, you'd glare as if you were mad at me. It was only when you were with Maddie that I got to see that charming guy again, the happy stranger I met in the grocery store," Gwen explained, earnestly.

It was self-preservation. He desperately wanted to explain, but how could he? Hearing how his behavior had looked from her point of view, his "preserved" self didn't feel any better. "If that's how I made you feel, I am sorry, but that's on me, not you," he said, nodding for emphasis. "You didn't do anything wrong. Of course I'm your friend. Always have been."

Unfortunately, friends was all they were, Reade later thought bitterly while he lay on the couch that night, his ears straining to hear her movements in his bedroom.

9

------

eade sat at a high-top table at a dingy roadside saloon one town over from East Dodge, restlessly waiting for one of his more litigious clients to stop propositioning some waitress near the bar and return with their drinks.

Garth Brooks' "Friends in Low Places" was playing. He tapped his fingers on the discolored Formica tabletop, thoughts drifting. Gwen wanted him to be her *friend*.

Yeah, that was how he wanted their relationship defined by the one woman he always wanted.

The innocent term set his teeth on edge. Reade had tried being her friend seven years ago, and it had nearly driven him out of his mind. The nicer he'd been to her, the brighter her smiles had gotten. The more he'd joked with her, the more she'd happily teased him back, and the deeper the knife in his gut had twisted. When, only a couple of months after her marriage, Gwen had told him that she was expecting a child, Reade had realized that he wasn't strong enough to keep it up. Maintaining a cool indifference when he was around her had kept him from feeling anything, a numbness he had come to live with for over half a decade. That numbness was now starting to painfully thaw, leaving Reade's emotions raw all over again.

Where is my frigging Scotch already? Reade wasn't happy to be at this seedy tavern to begin with, but at least that meant he had an excuse to have a drink in the middle of the afternoon. In an effort to keep the client happy, Reade had agreed to hold their quarterly check-in at the dive for a change. Tad Worth was the only son of a rich oil man, and being on retainer for his family kept half the office employed. If it wasn't a divorce or a DWI, it was another entanglement that Tad needed Reade and his staff to deal with.

Reade peered across the dimly lit room to see what was keeping Tad and the drinks. Apparently, the waitress was holding him captive. Future divorce number four for Tad? Reade couldn't see her face but could easily picture the type— curvaceous and calculating. This woman seemed to be on the tiny side, since Tad, who was several inches shorter than Reade, loomed over her. Though she was effectively blocked from Reade's line of vision, he could see that she had on the same barely there jumpsuit as the other female employees. It plunged down low and rode up high. Each young woman wore a different color, and the woman keeping Tad's attention was in teal. Tad had his arm extended and resting across a nearby pole, preventing Miss Teal from escaping. Or rather, the well-endowed Miss Teal. Reade couldn't help but notice—what man wouldn't? Thanks to the deep V halter neckline, little was left to the imagination.

Instead of admiring the view like Tad was obviously doing, Reade's mind drifted to Gwen in Sheila's nightshirt. Not that he needed much prompting to go there, as that image was constantly lurking in his mind. Reade was so hung up on Gwen that he could no longer look at another woman without thinking of her. *How pathetic.*

Reade refocused on the byplay between Tad and Miss Teal when the waitress tried dodging away from the arm blocking her path. Tad's other hand shot out and gripped her upper arm, successfully keeping her trapped while simultaneously drawing her closer to him. *Classy move*, Reade thought with a roll of his eyes. Where was the manager of this joint? Reade couldn't very well rescue the girl from his own client. No, he was simply going to go rescue his drink and see if he could interrupt the two in the process. He and Tad had work to discuss, anyway.

As Reade walked toward the bar, he heard *her* laugh. It was faint, but Reade could have sworn it was Gwen's laughter drifting through the stale room. It sent tingles up his spine. His senses now on high alert, Reade scanned the room, but he didn't see her familiar face. *What would Gwen be doing here, anyway?* The thought of her at this seedy dive bar had Reade derisively shaking his head. Look what being Gwen's "friend" was doing to him. Two weeks of living together and Reade was already starting to hear her laughter wherever he went. He was going to change his drink order to a double and no rocks.

Make it a triple, his mind screamed as Miss Teal successfully ducked and came up from under Tad's arm and into sight. Oh, Reade most assuredly knew that face. Every detail was already committed to his memory.

His lungs constricted. Forget teal; seeing Tad drooling all over *Gwen*, touching her, had Reade seeing red.

Gwen froze the moment she spotted Reade. His heated gaze held her glued to the spot. She could only stare back, watching the color of his gorgeous dark-brown eyes deepen to a midnight black as they narrowed at her.

Gulping, she looked around for somewhere to escape. *Where was a trap door when a girl needed one?* Bad enough she'd had to deal with the pawing of Mr. Scumbag these last few minutes, propositioning her to no end, she now had to be caught doing this demeaning job by Reade of all people.

Before either of them could speak from shock, Gwen was abruptly pulled back by the hem of her tiny shorts, into the waiting arms of Mr. Scumbag. While she'd had a few run-ins like these since she'd started working at the bar, never one with a customer who was so bold or insistent. Usually a harmless joke aimed at the man in question, accompanied by a wink, and Gwen was able to move on to the next table without too many ruffled feathers. She raised her elbow to give the guy a none-too-gentle jab to the stomach, but Reade's bellow stopped her in mid-action.

"Let go of her!"

Gwen flinched at the unexpected rage in his command.

"Walker, easy buddy," Mr. Scumbag said flippantly, barely glancing at Reade and instead keeping his eyes on her, or rather, her chest. The persistent customer continued to hold firmly, even when she tried to shrug him off. With a dismissive thrust of his finger, Mr. Scumbag pointed across the room, "Go find yourself another lucky charm from the rainbow of waitresses here."

"Reade, what are you doing here? Wait, you know this guy?" Gwen called out while trying harder to wiggle out of Mr. Scumbag's grip. He'd used Reade's last name.

"What am *I* doing here? What are *you* doing here, and dressed like—like, that?" Reade countered, looking angry.

Reade reached out, as if to catch her wrist, but Gwen had moved to cross her arms in a belated effort to cover herself. "What does it look like I'm doing here?" she threw back, now annoyed at both men.

"It *looks* like you're going home with me, right this minute," Reade demanded possessively.

Placing his arm around Gwen's shoulders, Mr. Scumbag

once again snatched her back against his side. "Whoa, I was just getting to the let's get out of here part, old man. I believe there's a saying: 'whatever the client wants, the client gets,' right?"

Mr. Scumbag slowly stroked her arm in a way that had Gwen wanting to gag, and made Reade look like he wanted to kill the guy. The creep added with a leer in her direction, "Sugar, I'm Tad Worth of Worth Oil. And don't let the name fool you, I'm 'worth' more than just a 'tad.'" He ended that nauseating introduction with a creepy laugh and a pucker of his thin lips.

Since he was apparently a client of Reade's, Gwen did her best to shift gears mentally. Holding back her revulsion as best she could, she rushed to alleviate the tension, to keep Reade from getting into any trouble professionally. Given Reade's menacing stare, she had no idea what he might say or do next. He was obviously mad as hell she hadn't been more upfront about her current job. *Not that it was any of his business.*

Looking back at Tad, she raced to think of a brush-off that would keep him at bay while also keeping her from being fired and Reade from losing some big oil client, too. Smiling up at Tad and batting her eyes in her best Scarlett O'Hara impression, Gwen said sweetly, "Hi Tad, I'm Gigi—" Nervously, she glanced at Reade. Would he give away her real identity? But he merely arched one dark eyebrow upon hearing the unexpected name. "And I'm not going anywhere with anyone, except over to table eight, which is waiting for me to take their order. I'll catch you boys later."

Before Gwen could make a grand exit, she hesitated, momentarily captivated by the muscle twitching along Reade's jaw. His cheek had started to pulse the moment she had started flirtatiously addressing Tad. She had no idea it could do that and was temporarily transfixed just looking back at him and his clenched jaw.

Until Tad chimed in, breaking Gwen out of her stupor. "I'll gladly give you my order, then. I order you to stay right here, sweet thing."

Sweet thing? Ugh, really? Gwen rolled her eyes and huffed out a breath of annoyance, calling for patience. Tad was really more than a "tad" much for her liking, so much so that she forgot to worry over Reade's anger, concentrating on her own rising irritation instead. "As much as I'd like to, I am not assigned to this area. Excuse me," she said, putting more force behind her words this time, and once again trying to shrug off Tad's roaming hands. Gwen didn't care if he was a client of Reade's or not, if he didn't back off, she was going to knee him in the groin.

"You can bet your boots that I can double whatever Walker has offered in the past," Tad said wolfishly, glancing back and forth between the two of them. "Hold on. She called you Reade. I thought you said you'd never been here before, Walker. How do you two know each other, anyway?"

Reade narrowed his eyes. There was a fire there, barely banked. It was exciting, but also had Gwen's nerves squirming in fear that he would lose his cool or do something that he might later regret in some misguided act of overprotectiveness.

"We are good friends," she quickly supplied taking control of the conversation. She had no idea what Reade had been about to say, but from the corner of her eye, she saw him flinch for some reason. Smiling over at him, she nodded, hoping he would confirm her statement. Instead, his jaw ticked again.

"We are more than 'friends,' actually. We live together," Reade said tightly, leveling Gwen with a stare that dared her to contradict him. "In fact, *Gigi* here is going to be sleeping in my bed tonight, isn't that right, babe?" Reade prodded, with a wickedly dangerous smile that both shocked her and made her heart flutter frantically.

Reade's deep voice, cocky smile, and the double meaning of

sleeping in his bed tonight caused a quick, thrilling shiver to run through her body. She had never seen him look quite so arousingly devilish, and she wasn't going to deny that she liked this edgier side of him. If this was how protectively he behaved with women, then Gwen was more envious of his exes than ever.

Remembering that she would be alone though in his king-sized bed made her even gloomier. She was about to clarify his misleading innuendo when she finally realized that he was giving her an easy out from the likes of Tad. She was happy to play along with the excuse he was offering her, but if he was going to be literal, then so be it. Two could play at this game, and no way was she letting the opportunity slip through her fingers.

"Uh, that's right, *babe.* I will be naked under your sheets, eagerly awaiting your touch," she purred, trying not to laugh at how both of Reade's brows lifted at her daring reply. If only he knew how honest her sarcastic confession really was.

He gave her a stern look. Perhaps she was pushing it too far. Pursing her lips and blowing Reade a kiss might have been a bit much, but she couldn't resist the opportunity. Take that! She was enjoying the freedom of actually being able to say what she was thinking, even if he thought she was only playacting.

Giving Reade her own wicked smile, Gwen walked over to him, taking advantage of the fact that Tad was too stunned to do anything about it. Or maybe Tad had also seen that dark look in Reade's eyes and mistaken Reade's anger at her as a threat toward him. Either way, it seemed as if Tad had finally decided to back off. Reade must have sensed the change too, because he immediately pulled her forward, next to him.

If she'd thought his angry stare was heated before, being up against Reade's side was practically setting her exposed skin on fire. His strong fingers resting intimately on her hip had her almost quivering. *Holy hell.*

"No shit?" Tad asked, reminding her of their audience. "Are you telling me that the same uptight lawyer who lectured me for marrying an exotic dancer in Vegas is shacked up with a waitress from a titty bar?" Laughing, Tad walked forward and slapped Reade on the back. "Maybe we have more in common, after all." Looking back at Gwen with a reluctant shake of his head, Tad added with a friendly nudge of his elbow, "If you ever get bored with this stuffed shirt, gimme a call. I promise to make it *worth* your while."

An ice cube's chance in hell, Gwen thought silently. Aloud, she said, "I really do have to get back to work." Not meeting Reade's heated glare, she couldn't help but play with fire a little more, so she teasingly stroked his bicep. "Bye, babe," she said, leaning up to give him a quick peck on his full lips. He gave her a heated look. Perhaps she had indeed pushed it too far now.

The chaste touch of his warm lips almost had her stumbling on wobbly legs as she hurriedly escaped, fleeing to her assigned table of college guys who were waiting for her to finally take their order.

Once she was halfway across the room, Reade called out to her, "Gigi, I'll see you at home, sweet thing."

With him throwing back the term Tad had used earlier, combined with the use of her alias, it didn't take a detective to figure out that she was in for more questions and explanations "at home."

Damn. She'd known better than to have played with fire. *This is exactly what my snowballing disaster of a life needs right now.*

∾

Reade stayed at the bar for another hour, sipping his drink and talking with his client. Gwen spotted them briefly reviewing papers while seated on the rickety stools along the wooden teak bar, but for the most part, Reade mostly glared at her whenever she walked by or looked his way.

Well, he could go ahead and judge her all he wanted. Reade wasn't the one trying to climb up from rock bottom and provide for a child at the same time. Dignity and humility no longer had a place in her life right now.

A younger waitress in a red jump suit, who simply went by the name Red, was darkening Gwen's mood further. Red was currently fawning all over Reade, laughing and tossing back her shiny midnight-black hair in a come-hither manner, before brazenly playing with his slim necktie.

That's not even Red's assigned station. Gwen considered pulling the girl's thick mane and dragging her over to the area where she was supposed to be working. Instead, she threw Tony—the bartender, manager, and owner—a pointed look with a nod toward Red, but all he did was give her a thumbs-up in return.

What did I expect? Tony had, not so subtly, indicated that Gwen should be "friendly" with the customers, too. She wasn't going to get any help from him, and she certainly didn't expect smarmy Tad to intervene.

To Gwen's shock, Tad did just that, eagerly pulling Red to his side instead. He whispered something in her ear that had Red laughing with delight instead of revulsion. Gwen could have almost hugged Tad for being a horny creep at that moment.

When it finally came time for Gwen to punch out, Reade was suddenly by her side again. He silently followed her out the door and to her car, presumably to keep up their relationship pretense for Tad's sake. Reade needn't have bothered, though. With Red sitting firmly on Tad's lap, fiddling with his collar, the bar could have been held up by armed robbers and Tad wouldn't have noticed. She let out a disgusted snort. Gwen couldn't imagine a more apropos couple.

Reade remained brooding once outside, not saying a word as he held open her car door then forcefully shutting it behind her and turning to walk to his own ride. His black SUV followed behind her on the drive back to his home.

Will he head back to work or follow me upstairs?

Hopefully the latter. Gwen only had a half hour before Maddie's school bus arrived. Then again, she'd prefer to have their argument over and done with before then. Defeated, Gwen entered the apartment with Reade right on her heels and braced herself for his questions.

Apparently, the second the door slammed behind them wasn't too soon for Reade who was now looming over her with an intensity in his eyes that surprised her. "*That* was your new 'food services' job? No wonder you've been leaving each day in a damned coat in this heat. I could tell you were embarrassed, but figured you were employed at some food chain or a school cafeteria or something. The idea of you working at a strip club never even entered my mind," Reade ranted.

"I didn't lie," Gwen pointed out, defiantly. "And you know it's *not* a strip club!"

He simply glared at her for a moment, his arms folded across his large chest. "How could you let some stranger touch you and stare at you?"

Sighing, Gwen started to take off her trench coat but, thinking better of it, pulled the belt tighter. The skimpy jumpsuit underneath would only provide a vivid reminder of just how degrading her new job was. "You think I like it? You think guys like Tad don't make my skin crawl? I have a master's degree, and the only job I could get around here was as a waitress, parading around in a barely there costume! Do you know how demoralizing that is?"

"Then why do it?" he asked, following her.

"You know why!" Gwen yelled, throwing up her hands but just barely checking the impulse to childishly stomp her foot at his obtuseness. "I need the money so Maddie and I can get out of here. No one in town will hire me now. In New York, I can take back my maiden name, and no one will know the difference in a city of over eight million people."

With a deep exhale, his shoulders seemed to lose some of their earlier rigidity. "I'll give you the money you need, or provide a personal loan if you'd rather. You don't have to do this. You know I'd make sure you and Maddie were taken care of."

"Don't you understand that I already feel pathetic taking over your home and depending on you like this? And if there's one thing I've learned from Jesse leaving, it's that I don't want to have to depend on anyone ever again."

"This is crazy," Reade said, grabbing her shoulders as if he was resisting shaking some sense into her. Still, he seemed to be calming down more, his voice softening. "You said you wanted me to be your friend, then let me be your friend and help you. No strings attached."

"You're already helping by letting us stay here until the school year is out. Thank you," she responded, letting herself sink into his grip.

"I don't want you to thank me," he growled, getting worked up again. "I want you to quit working there." He slid his hands to her upper arms and squeezed a bit before quickly pulling away completely to lean on the side of the sofa.

"No," Gwen said stubbornly, perversely missing his touch, while still being so mad she felt like pushing him off the arm rest. "Not until I can save up some money on my own. Even if I took a loan from you, I would still need to pay it back."

"I don't care if you ever pay it back. I have the money, and I won't have you prostituting yourself for tips," Reade threw out, his voice rising again in agitation as he pushed away from the couch.

Gwen's breath came out in a hiss. "I'd slap you for that if I didn't know how ridiculous that comparison is. It's hardly come to that, Reade. Most of the time it's just like any waitressing job." With a frustrated sigh, she ripped her coat off anyway and marched toward his bedroom.

Blood rushed straight to Reade's groin as he stared at Gwen's retreating backside, outlined perfectly by the skintight material of her jumpsuit. He swore under his breath.

Not bothering to turn to look at him, she threw over her shoulder, "I have to change before Maddie gets home. Thank you for your concern, but I'll be fine." Gwen's voice faltered for a second, and her purposeful stride came to a brief halt. "I am sorry that I didn't tell you where I was working, but really it wouldn't have made a difference."

"Hell," Reade mumbled, as she slammed the door to his bedroom in his face. He had only meant to rile her with that low-blow prostitution comment, to get her as mad as he was, but it only seemed to make her sad. He knew he was acting like an ass. After all, who was he to demand she quit? He had no say in the matter.

On one hand, he was proud of her for standing her ground and pushing back, but on the other, he wished it wasn't against him. If only he could calm down and get the images of her in that sexy outfit and that seedy bar out of his mind. To think, he had been getting all hot and bothered over seeing her in a baggy robe. Meanwhile, for the last couple of weeks, any old drunk jerk had gotten to look his fill? Thank goodness Gwen had only been working the afternoon shifts, not at night, when all walks of life would visit that dive.

The other waitresses were more experienced and harder. They knew how to handle themselves. Gwen could barely escape a spoiled rich guy. It had taken all of Reade's willpower to keep from yanking Tad's wandering hands off of Gwen's scantily clad body and using them to beat his client to a bloody pulp.

Recalling the incident had Reade worked up all over again and pacing his living room. It didn't help when he realized that this Saturday was Gwen's evening shift, and she would be working late while Maddie was having a sleepover. The same night that he was going out to dinner regarding the Barcelona deal. His partners were even coming in from New York and Los Angeles to join the celebration.

There was no way Reade could get out of it. No, he had to figure out a way to get *Gigi* to change her mind.

10

"Call in sick," Reade suggested one last time as Gwen slipped her trench coat on over the ridiculous spandex jumpsuit. Based on her resolute stance, this wasn't a case he was going to win. He had to try one last closing argument, though. "The afternoons are just a bunch of college kids and working guys blowing off steam on their lunch hour, but the men going late at night are real dirtbags. Too drunk to care if they're inappropriate. That's why they're there, looking for some easy action that they can't find by themselves."

"Well, I'm not easy, so they'll be disappointed," Gwen huffed.

"You know that's not what I meant. And guys like that don't handle disappointment well," he reasoned.

"Reade, I can handle myself. I'm a New Yorker, remember?" she responded.

He snorted. "You can hardly compare the upper crust New York suburbs to the mean streets of the Big Apple, or to this dirtbag playground."

Gwen ignored that jab. "Maddie is sleeping over at her

friend Becca's house. I have the number and address on the fridge, just in case."

"What about the paparazzi?" Reade asked, grasping at straws now. "What happens if someone recognizes you? Imagine that story."

"I was worried about that at first, but the men that go in there aren't up on the latest political affairs, and I hardly look like a senator's wife in this outfit and caked-on makeup. Just in case, I go by the name Gigi. Gwen Gallo, G-G, get it?"

He didn't reply, but continued to frown silently at her.

"Well, I thought it was pretty clever." She pouted. "Don't worry, it will all make for fun commentary in my future set-the-record-straight story. Even the acclaimed Gloria Steinem was a Playboy Bunny waitress once."

"A bunny costume would be a classy step up in comparison to your getup. For crying out loud, the name of the damn place is Double D's Breastaurant!"

He had to go there, didn't he? She couldn't very well defend that blasted name, and she was tired of having the same argument anyway. Reade had been trying to convince her to quit ever since he'd discovered her at work three days ago. He'd brought it up again after her meeting with Danielle, too. She half expected him to camp out in the bar tonight.

Although the knowledge that Reade cared enough to become protective of her was heady indeed, Gwen couldn't get past the thought that Reade really must believe her to be helpless. *How pathetic I must seem to him.*

"You know, I would be there tonight if I could," he said. "But I agreed weeks ago to tonight's client dinner to toast, so to speak, the liquor deal I closed in Barcelona. If my partners weren't coming in from out of town, I would blow it off."

"Don't be ridiculous, go to work. I do not need a bodyguard or a lawyer, Reade. I'll see you in the morning."

With that, his teal-clad bunny hopped out his front door.

The apartment was blessedly dark and quiet when Gwen got home that night, or rather that morning. It was a little after two a.m., and she wasn't up for bickering with Reade again, especially when she felt so defeated.

Working the Saturday night shift at Double D's Breastaurant had been even creepier than Reade had suggested, and Gwen was fed up and embarrassed. She would have quit, but now she felt like she had something to prove, not to mention the tips she was pocketing were finally starting to add up. It wouldn't be much longer before she could afford to move.

Being in this in-between state sucked, but despite the chaos of the last month, it was nice being able to spend so much time with Reade, even if it was temporary. She looked forward to seeing him every morning and wishing him a good night each evening.

His apartment was comfortable, and it buoyed her spirits coming back to it. Of course it wasn't the physical apartment, so much as knowing she was in Reade's world, which left her feeling happy each day. Despite her terrible job.

Maddie had adjusted quite easily, too, which made things even more bittersweet. Her sweet girl was just as eager to see Reade when he got home, always running to greet him. Jesse used to be away for a month at a time, if not longer, yet Gwen couldn't recall a time when Maddie ran into his arms in welcome. Not that he'd ever bothered to extend his arms out to her. But that nightly ritual would be ending soon; school let out in just one more week.

Gwen feared Maddie would take the news about leaving

even worse than she had originally. Moving was the only thing that Maddie had objected to after hearing about her dad. But even though Reade had never complained about having them around, he had to be looking forward to getting his bachelor pad back.

Tiptoeing into the unlit apartment, Gwen managed to make it down the hall to the master bathroom without too much noise. Once inside, she quickly peeled off the horrid jumpsuit, washed up, and slipped into her borrowed nightshirt. Entering the connecting bedroom, she quietly closed the door behind her and turned on the lights, only to come to an abrupt stop.

Shocked, Gwen did a double take. Reade lay on top of the bed, fully dressed and sound asleep. Had he forgotten that she was staying here? Was he passed out drunk? She sniffed the air around him but did not detect the familiar stench of alcohol, which reeked off of most of the guys at the bar.

Should I wake him? No. This was his bed, after all. She would just go sleep on the pullout couch, like Reade had been doing the last few weeks. Or she could sleep in the den, since Maddie was away tonight. It was late. She should leave Reade be, but she couldn't help steal a moment, to just watch him breathing peacefully.

His powerful chest rose and fell beneath his suit and knotted tie. He didn't look very comfortable. Gwen smirked. She had no choice but to take off his tie and jacket. For his sake, obviously. What kind of friend would she be if she left him like that?

A smart one.

After the night she'd just had, she deserved this little indulgence, and really, where was the harm in helping out a friend? Softly walking up to the bed, Gwen whispered Reade's name, making sure she wasn't about to get caught semi-undressing him. Sliding her hands under his jacket over his hard muscles and up toward his broad shoulders, she gently peeled back the fabric of the coat. Holding her breath, she slipped his left arm out of one sleeve, then the right out of the other and eased the jacket out from under him. Reade swayed slightly toward her for a second, but then settled back into place.

She glanced up at his face, to check if she had woken him, but he remained motionless. Relieved, she let herself breathe again and continued on, gently loosening Reade's red silken tie from its precise knot. Pulling on one end of the unknotted tie, Gwen slowly slipped it free and placed it on the bedside table, running the silky scrap of fabric between her fingers.

Mesmerized with simply staring at his sleeping face, she admired Reade's strong jaw with its slight, dark stubble, which only made him look even more enticing. She couldn't stop herself from brushing her fingers lightly up his jawline. His thick, lush lips put her thinner ones to shame. She would love to press her lips to his and see how they fit, but that would definitely be crossing the line into creepy territory.

Do I dare unbutton his collar? The top button, under his neck, did look awfully tight, and before she could talk herself out of it, Gwen's fingers moved toward it. She had just freed the stiff button, when suddenly, she was pulled down on top of him. Her body flattened against his chest, shockingly hard beneath hers. Without the slightest warning, their positions reversed. She was drawn under him, his weight pinning her into the soft mattress.

Reade was above her, and his lips, the ones she had just been hungrily staring at, found hers. His mouth was so rough and warm, Gwen couldn't help but suck and taste him, all thoughts gone.

11

*A*s soon as he arrived home, Reade went into the bedroom to see if Gwen had returned safe and sound. Throughout dinner, it had taken all of his control to pay attention to the guests around him and resist the urge to drive to the bar and check on her. No, rather: carry her out of the bar caveman style and back to the safety of his home, despite her protests.

One of his partners had actually had to nudge him to make him respond to the client. That was just one of several times he'd had to ask someone to repeat themselves during the course of the meal. Besides worrying over Gwen, Reade had been the only one at the dinner without a spouse or a significant other. He couldn't help but fantasize about how great it would have been to have had Gwen with him, as his date. He'd have proudly introduced her to everyone, and not as a mere "friend."

When he realized that Gwen was not back yet, Reade sat down on the corner of his bed to read a couple of work emails on his phone.

He must have fallen asleep though, because the next thing

he knew, Gwen was trailing her hands up his chest. Teasing and torturing him by removing his suitcoat and tie. Her actions might not have been intentionally seductive, but they were driving him wild.

The fact that she had not realized that he was awake was beyond Reade's comprehension. Maybe he should have gone into a career as an actor. Surely if he could manage to stay still for as long as he had, then he deserved to win an award.

For a moment, it seemed like she was going to stop at taking off his tie, but Reade silently urged her to keep going, burning for more of her touch. When he risked a peek through his lowered lashes, Gwen was intensely staring at his lips, and he had to stifle his groan.

Was she interested in a kiss? If so, he was more than happy to oblige. The thought had his blood racing. When he realized Gwen was going to unbutton his shirt next, he had to take advantage of his sudden stroke of luck. Did he dare?

Hell, yes.

He might never get a chance like this again, and he was about to test the water—or rather *taste*. He wasn't gentle as he claimed her mouth, owning it like it belonged to him, finally.

Pushing against Reade's chest, Gwen turned her head away, pulling her lips from his and gasping for air. "Reade, stop!" she urged.

Does he think I'm someone else? She couldn't handle being just a stand-in. "Wake up, Reade, you're dreaming."

Reade seemed to find her frantic words funny, and his low laugh vibrated through their connected bodies. "Oh, I am most definitely awake. In fact, all of me is," he said with a sensual smile. "I'd be more than happy to pinch you to prove that it's not a dream, if you'd like. I even have a particular spot in mind."

Gwen's gaze flew to Reade's in disbelief. "Have you been drinking?" she asked, startled.

"Yes," he mumbled, moving down to kiss her neck.

"Are you drunk?" she asked.

"It depends," he hedged, licking the hollow of her throat.

"On what?" Gwen wondered, gritting her teeth. He was being deliberately evasive.

"On how you react," Reade responded, a grin pulling at his luscious lips, before once again sweeping his tongue inside her mouth to sensuously tangle with hers.

"How I react to what?" she asked, frustrated with his vague responses but unable to stop her moan as they broke apart. The weight of his body pressing her into the mattress was causing further frustration on an even more basic level.

"This," Reade said, covering her mouth for another wild kiss. A kiss that stole Gwen's breath away. Her body took over. She'd fantasized about this for so long, and she wanted to revel in the feel of their bodies moving together…

But her mind refused to let her enjoy the moment. She pushed him away, whimpering at the sudden break in contact. "Seriously, you don't *really* want me," she exhaled shakily. "You're half asleep, and I won't be just a convenient body, and I don't want you to regret this in the morning."

"Want you?" Reade taunted, his amused look now intensely serious. "Don't you dare talk to me about wanting. I've wanted you from the first moment I saw you, and, believe me, it's been far from convenient. My only regret is not doing this sooner."

Vehemently shaking her head, Gwen tried to break free from Reade's hold and his oh-so-tempting explanation. "You can't possibly mean that. Half the time, I still think you don't even like me."

"You're right, I don't like you," he snapped, and Gwen felt the blow of his words directly in the pit of her stomach before splintering up toward her battered heart.

"See?" she whimpered. Not wanting him to see her cry, Gwen shoved against Reade's broad chest trying to sit up, but he would not budge.

"Gwen," Reade said gruffly, looking into her eyes and holding her to him firmly. "*Like* does not begin to describe how I feel about you. I have been in love with you from day one."

Biting her bottom lip, Gwen shook her head again, not daring to believe what he was saying. *How could that possibly be true?*

"You don't believe me?" Reade asked, emitting a brief, unhappy-sounding chuckle. "Here I've been afraid that you would find out a million different times how crazy I am about you, and the whole time, you've thought that I don't like you? Far from it. I don't like cars; the only reason I used to help Jesse work on that damned Vette was to see you. To be near you. I don't even like Jesse, for that matter. In fact, I can't stand the entitled bastard. I've turned down offers to run larger firms in bigger markets, because I couldn't bear being that far away from you."

Gwen's heart skipped a beat at his words, and her head was spinning, but how could she believe him? He was probably just caught up in the moment. *It's better if I don't say anything. Then I won't get hurt. Again.* It might be cowardly, but she didn't want to risk everything when there was a chance that Reade might come to his senses. She didn't think she'd survive it.

Reade's dark eyes bore into hers, questioning, and his hands roamed restlessly up and down her body. She shivered with pleasure. Abruptly, he squeezed her to him and ground out, "Fuck it, tonight I don't care if you're Jesse's girl, I can't take it anymore. I want you so badly, I can't even think straight."

She was already lifting her lips toward his for the passionate kiss she expected to follow his heated words when, instead, she heard him grumble, "Where did you put my damn tie?"

Gwen was dumbfounded. "What? Your tie? Why?" *He better not be planning on getting dressed and leaving.*

"I am a desperate man, and now that I finally have you in my bed, I want to make sure you don't leave it. I'm willing to tie you up if I have to. Because finally, I want to know what it feels like to make love to the woman I've loved for so long."

Evidently giving up his search for the tie, Reade pulled Gwen's arms up over her head instead, pinning her wrists with his hands as he went to work on his plan, starting by trailing kisses along the base of her throat, then diving lower, into her cleavage.

"I want to explore every inch of you, taste you, touch you, memorize every detail, every sigh, every moan," he murmured, looking up from his exploration of her body to stare at her through hooded eyes clouded with passion. "If you don't want this, Gwen, please tell me now. But if you stay with me, baby, I promise to make this an evening we will never forget."

She wasn't really expected to answer that just then, was she? Gwen was so overcome with ecstatic delight over Reade's words and the feel of his mouth tracing her collarbone that she couldn't speak. She wanted this night just as badly as he did. Damn the consequences and the questions that would surface tomorrow.

Unable to form a coherent response, she nodded. Evidently that was all the confirmation he needed. His eyes instantly lit with triumph. "Thank God," he said, shoving his hands roughly into her hair and thrilling her with a scorching kiss.

He slid one arm beneath her, gathering her by the waist and drawing her body tight against his. Within seconds Gwen was burning for him, need filling her.

He pulled her nightshirt up and over her head in one swift movement, his eyes greedily raking down her body. For a second, Gwen was nervous under such scrutiny. No one had seen her naked in a very long time. But Reade's appreciative smile made her feel sexy, alleviating her shyness.

"Damn, you're gorgeous," Reade stated, his voice husky. "You're even more beautiful than I imagined," he whispered almost reverently.

Seconds passed like hours as Reade's heated gaze roamed over her body.

When waiting for his caress became too much, she demanded, "Touch me."

He nodded eagerly in agreement with a wicked smile, as if he knew something she didn't. The palms of his hands scraped against her sensitive nipples as he slid his fingers over her flesh to cup her generous breasts. When he gently tweaked her hardened buds then soothingly laved each one with his tongue, she arched her back in hungry response. Her body was ready to incinerate, and they'd barely gotten started.

And as for exploring every inch of her, Reade did that, too. Including the surprisingly sensitive underside of her knee, which he bit and then soothed with his tongue.

Gwen found it unbearably sexy when he mumbled her name and cursed with pleasure as he let her push him on his back to undo the rest of the buttons of his tailored dress shirt. She had her own fantasies to sate, after all, and she was not about to be outdone.

Gently, she nipped at his ear and let her hands caress his wide chest, fascinated by the smooth ruggedness of him. She needed to feel more, feel everything. Sliding her body over his, she marveled at the sensation of her nipples brushing his hot skin. Achingly slow, she traveled down to the waistband of his pants.

"You're killing me, love." he passionately swore, sounding like he was at the end of his control. "I need to get out of these pants."

And into me, Gwen thought desperately.

Enjoying being in command, though, she flashed him a saucy grin before slowly undoing the button of his pants and sliding down his zipper. Keeping her eyes locked on his passion-filled eyes, Gwen slipped her hand inside his briefs to grab hold of his swollen cock. Now it was Reade's turn to arch off the bed, as he involuntarily thrust his hips up to rub his thick shaft against her greedy hand.

Before she could explore more, Reade shed the rest of his clothes, removing his pants and briefs in one fluid motion.

Leaning over him, Gwen took her time to stare at his gorgeous body, focusing on one area in particular. When she licked her lips and began to lean her head down, Reade roughly grabbed her hips and rolled her onto her back again.

Shaking his head, he let out a pained chuckle. "Rain check, sweetheart," he huffed. "If you put that gorgeous mouth on him now, I won't last, and I need to be inside you. Now."

With that delicious pronouncement, Reade snaked his hand down between Gwen's legs, urging her to open for him. Smoothing his hand over her mound, he explored her heat. All of his fingers worked simultaneously to torture her aching sex. He slipped his fingers between her wet folds, circling, spreading her moisture, inflaming them both. Gwen reveled in his skilled touch, and how he seemed to know exactly how much pressure to exert on her throbbing nub, moving from a steady to a rapid pace. Too soon, she felt her whole body start to vibrate, her belly tightening.

"No fair, you didn't let me touch you," Gwen protested weakly, trying to delay her impending orgasm by attempting to push his hand away and clench her thighs together. Reade ignored her paltry efforts, skillfully continuing to pleasure her, changing his movements and direction, spreading her legs farther apart. When Gwen finally relaxed, giving in to his insistence, Reade tormented her further, stroking from her entrance to her clit, then lightly circling and teasing it.

Gwen moaned as Reade slowly slid a finger inside her, thrusting and retreating several times before adding a second, while still using his thumb to caress her swollen clit. "Oh, God. Reade. Please."

"Tell me what you want, baby," he said huskily.

"You. I want *you*," Gwen moaned brokenly. She peered into his eyes as he brought his lips down to hers, before dueling with his demanding tongue as he plunged it in and out of her mouth, mimicking the movement of his fingers at her core.

The spiral in her belly started to unfurl, tension spreading to every part of her body. Reade had worked her up so much with his delicious touch that Gwen lost her control entirely. She had wanted to say more, to tell Reade where she wanted him, and how, but the volcanic climax took her by surprise and rippled over her body in pulsating waves of blinding-hot intensity.

Reade pulled his fingers from between her legs and took a deep breath before letting it out slowly. The heated rush of his exhale drifted over her hypersensitive skin. Still floating blissfully as her quivering abated, she watched him make an effort to calm himself.

In between ragged breaths, Reade said in a voice filled with awe, "You feel so good. That was the sexiest thing I've ever seen. Better than I ever imagined, and believe me, I've imagined this often."

So have I. And she was ready for more of the reality. Slightly embarrassed from her unguarded response, Gwen was determined he feel just as glorious. Reaching down, she stroked the velvety, strong length of his cock, marveling at the way his body shuddered with her every touch and movement.

Reade made an inarticulate sound of need and rolled on top of her.

Stilling for a second, he reached off to the side of his bed and pulled open the top drawer of his nightstand to grab a foil packet. Ripping the package open with his teeth, he stared into her eyes, possibly in question.

Not wanting any further delay, Gwen reached for the condom and helped unroll it over his straining cock. She guided him inside her, loving the feel of him filling her, stretching her. He entered her with a curse of pleasure. Teeth clenched, Reade groaned her name, his hooded eyes smoldering.

They glided together for what seemed like forever. Each time Reade seemed close to finding his release, he would shift positions and start building toward it all over again. Gwen couldn't believe his stamina and control, especially when she was about to lose hers all over again. As a test, she pushed her hips forward rapidly, and Reade hissed. It made her feel powerful, knowing she could cause that strong of a reaction in him.

Tempting his restraint, she took over the rhythm, making it faster, harder, and wilder. Delighting in Reade's now equally frantic movements, she pushed her hips higher, rocking into his demanding thrusts until, finally, they shattered in unison.

Gwen's heartbeat was thundering in her ears, but she still managed to hear his heated shout of release. "Fuck, yes!" Reade exclaimed in her ear, followed by a low groan that was almost guttural, sending a new set of chills through her.

Until that blissful moment, Gwen didn't believe coming at the same time was actually possible, outside of the claims in steamy novels.

I'll be damned, they had it right. She buried her satisfied smile in Reade's chest, unable to stop herself from savoring his salty skin with another taste and a quick love bite in the process.

Neither he nor she said a word after, just holding each other for a while, occasionally kissing a spot of bare flesh that would cross their paths, until eventually, they couldn't stay still any longer. They made love once more, then finally fell asleep in each other's arms, only to wake before dawn and start again.

12

I'm having that dream again, Gwen thought, floating awake. This time it was different, though. And then, remembering, she came fully awake with a smile. *This is real.*

Feeling Reade's strong body along her back, spooning her in a loose embrace, his heavy arm casually slung around her hip, Gwen couldn't help but sigh with contentment. She was finally in his arms, and somehow, he'd been as crazy about her as she'd been about him, all these years.

What now? A million insecure questions started flooding her mind, poking holes into her early morning happiness. Was this just a getting-it-out-of-his-system type of thing?

She had remained silent long enough. *It's now or never. What's the worst that can happen? I don't end up with Reade? I'm not really with him now, I've just been playing house for the last few weeks. Time to find out what's real. No more regrets.*

Turning onto her side to face him, she found Reade fully awake and giving her a satisfied smirk that was sexy as hell. His hair was sexily mussed, and she wanted to reach out and run her hands through it as she did last night.

She watched him for a moment longer, worrying about

ruining his smile of contentment but not wanting to hide anything from him anymore. *I love this man.* The feeling was so unlike the last time she'd given her heart away that this time she was sure of how she felt and could see the difference. Breaking the silence, Gwen took a deep breath and started to test the waters. "I have to tell you something."

Hmm, maybe I should have started off with "good morning." Fortunately, Reade didn't seem to mind her directness. In fact, he looked like he was trying not to laugh at her for it.

"You can tell me anything," he said, his voice even sexier when it was rough with sleep. Leaning toward her, he playfully nipped her bottom lip.

Encouraged, Gwen returned his love bite but pulled back before he could deepen it into a full kiss. She needed to tell him how she felt and, hopefully, wouldn't jeopardize whatever this was in the process.

She wasn't sure how or where to start and briefly wished that Reade had still been asleep, so she could have had a moment to rehearse exactly what she wanted to say. Concentrating on Reade's lazy smile, she dove in mid-thought, a terrible nervous habit of hers. "Jesse wasn't the only one who cheated."

And just like that, there went Reade's smile. "What?" he asked, his furrowed brows betraying his confusion. "You had an affair?"

"No." Gwen stumbled over her words, trying to get her explanation out quickly. "Not physically, but...emotionally, perhaps. Jesse said I was holding back from him and that it was driving him crazy. He claimed it was one of the reasons that he wanted separate bedrooms. I figured that it was just another excuse that he made up to cut me out of his life, to make me feel like a bad wife, but later, I had to admit to myself that he was right. I had been caring for someone else the whole time we'd been married."

. . .

Her words were strangling his heart.

Just great. Reade released a litany of curses in his mind. Now he was jealous of someone he had never met. Or did he know the bastard? Her college friend in New York?

Too bad. Gwen was finally in his bed, and he was never going to let her go.

He couldn't very well demand the name of this mystery guy. And to be honest, while he frantically wanted to know who the bastard was, he was afraid to find out. If Gwen was going to be with someone other than Jesse, Reade was determined that it had to be him. He couldn't go through seeing her with someone else, loving someone else. Not again.

He'd already despised knowing Gwen had been just as unhappy as he had been during her marriage, but knowing she had longed for someone else entirely made his chest ache and his fists clench. His eyebrows drew together. "So, why didn't you go to him? This lover? When you were down and out, why didn't you call him for help? Offer him a proposition?" he snapped out, pulling away and turning his back, needing space between them.

If he was acting like a sulky child, so be it. And like a child, he couldn't help but feel that she was his now, and he was not going to share. *Mine!* The word kept running through his mind like a vow. He wanted all of her, dammit. Patiently, he waited to hear her response, so he could formulate his case to keep her. Forever.

"He was *not* my lover, not then," Gwen qualified, "but, I did call him, and he offered his support, without me even asking."

"Of course he did," Reade grumbled.

Gwen ignored his interruption and continued, "He said Maddie and I could live with him."

Over my fucking dead body. He tried his best to bite his words back before he said something he could not take back. Once again, though, he didn't take his own advice. Instead, he growled, "Then why aren't you with this knight in shining armor now?"

"Who says I'm not?" Gwen asked, stroking the tense muscles of his turned back. Scooting closer, she wrapped her arms around him, tenderly kissing his shoulder. "It's you. It's always been you."

It took Reade a few moments to see beyond his jealousy and fully take in the life-altering meaning of what she had just said. Still, he was almost afraid to hope.

"Gwen," he demanded, his voice deep with suppressed emotion, "are you saying what I think you're saying?"

"I love you," she confessed proudly.

Like a pouncing tiger, Reade had Gwen under him before she could even complete her startled gasp. He brushed a rushed kiss across her lips, then trailed his mouth down her neck and sucked at the hollow of her throat. Sliding one arm beneath her, he gathered her by the waist, crushing her body tight against his.

Bracing himself above her on one arm, Reade looked down at Gwen's amused face. He wanted to believe her sweet confession, but he needed to hear her confirm it. "Gwen, you don't have to pretend that all these years you felt the same way. I'm just glad you do now."

"It's the truth, Reade. I was attracted to you from the moment we met, or rather the moment you caught me, but you never seemed to show any real interest. You were so kind and easygoing in the beginning, and I hoped you felt the connection too, but you never said anything, and I've never been the type to make the first move," Gwen explained.

"How could I make a move? You were already dating Jesse and writing your infamous exposé on him. The next thing I knew, your legendary romance was all over the news. How could I compete with that?"

"We had just gone on a date or two at that point, nothing official. I wasn't sure if I was even interested in him or just had a case of hero worship. After the trip to Dodge, though, he was relentless, with one romantic gesture after another. Being pursued by him felt like a roller coaster ride. And I never had the chance to stop it or see straight."

"If you weren't sure, then why the hell did you marry him?"

"I wanted something stable in my life, a family. I think I was vulnerable and a little bit lost after my parents died, and he knew I was someone he could control. Now I can see I was an easy mark for a persuasive man like him. Besides, he was the only one throwing his hat in the ring, so I let myself get caught up in the fantasy of it all." Shaking her head with remorse, she continued, "And I thought that Jesse loved me, so I told myself that my interest in you wasn't realistic. I chalked it up to cold feet and figured it would be stupid to throw away a future on a one-sided what-if."

"I wish you had said something," he said gruffly after a moment.

Gwen shot him an incredulous look. "Me? What about you? The week before we went to City Hall, I straight out asked you if I should marry Jesse and if I was making the right choice, remember?"

"Of course I remember. And it nearly killed me to tell you to listen to your heart and then see you marry the jerk anyway. I thought you came to me as a friend and were simply looking for advice, not a declaration. All I wanted to do was list every bad quality of Jesse's, but I thought you were so in love with him that it would make me look vindictive and jealous. Believe me, I've revisited that moment lots of times over the years, and each time I've envisioned different endings, from kidnapping to shaking you and forcing you to choose *me*." Reade pointed his thumb toward his chest.

"Well, it turned out not to matter," Gwen said solemnly. "The day after we talked, I found out I was pregnant, and then there was no going back."

They were quiet for a moment, both of them taking it all in.

"All this time, I thought it was only my heart breaking," Gwen said, lovingly reaching up to touch Reade's cheek.

A few tears slipped out of her eyes. Reade brought his hands up to cradle her face, brushing her tears away with his thumbs, mesmerized by how her green eyes turned a shade darker when she cried. Hopefully he'd be able to stare into her eyes forever, but they would rarely be obscured by tears. "Shh," Reade soothed. "That won't do us any good, baby. At least we're together now, finally. That's what matters."

Sighing, Gwen turned her head and kissed his palm. After wiping the rest of her tears away, she gave him a feeble smile. "You're right, and I wouldn't change having Maddie for anything, so it must have been meant to be. But I'm so glad it's not just my heart alone in this anymore."

Reade kissed her with all the longing he'd felt over the years. "Me, too. It will never be just yours again, not if I can help it."

"Promise?" Gwen asked.

"I promise. You're my girl, now. Forever."

13

---

*F*rustrated, Reade reread the same legalese paragraph for the fifth time. It had turned dark outside over an hour ago, and yet he was still stuck in his office on the second floor. Cursing, he slapped the paperwork across his desk, irritated that he hadn't absorbed a single detail and wishing he was upstairs with Gwen and Maddie. Damn, if they weren't addictive.

They had always been lurking in the corners of his mind before, but now he kept craning his ears to hear their footsteps through the ceiling above, which wasn't helping him get his work done any faster. Maddie was probably getting ready for bed, and he wouldn't have a chance to say goodnight or check over her homework with her. No, he was stuck finalizing a contract that needed to be sent over to his client, pronto.

Sadly, he probably still had another hour before he could comfortably sign off on it. The stupid thing should have been finalized hours ago. Instead, Reade had spent the better part of the afternoon tangled up in the sheets with Gwen. He had snuck away from his files and surprised her upstairs once she got back from her shift. Remembering that brought a slow, satisfied grin to his face. Unfortunately, the memory also managed to make his pants tight.

So now, here he was, making up for the time he'd lost earlier, and growing quite uncomfortable in the process. Reade had made his bed, so to speak, and he'd gladly sleep in it—as long as Gwen was in it with him. Sighing, he retrieved the file, straightening the papers into a semblance of order, and tried to reread the highlighted clause once more. Maybe if he really concentrated, he could be done in a half hour and could finally go home to his girls. That was the incentive he needed to focus.

Or maybe, he could text Gwen and ask her to come down and join him for a bit. That way, he could finally entertain his fantasy of taking her right there on his large mahogany desk.

In the past, just seeing Gwen in his office had him wishing she was laid out on top of it with him between her spread legs. It had gotten to the point that he'd been forced to move their Literary Foundation meetings to the boardroom, with his staff present. Now, he didn't have to control himself. The last week with Gwen was better than anything he'd imagined all those years. With a smirk, he let himself revel in the images that were no longer just fantasies.

A moment later, Reade was sure that he was still daydreaming, when he caught sight of Gwen standing in the doorway to his office, a baby monitor clipped on the waistband of her hip. His sour mood lifted immediately at just the sight of her.

"Can I come in?" she asked, her sultry voice shooting an electric jolt through him.

Reade nodded, too caught off guard to speak. Admiring the sassy swing of her hips as she rounded his desk, he held his breath. Then she slung her hip up to rest on the very surface where he had just been picturing her naked.

With a suppressed groan, he pushed the images aside. Still,

he couldn't resist reaching out and possessively placing his hand on her thigh, to make sure she was really there.

Will I ever get tired of looking at her, touching her? He certainly hoped not.

"Am I bothering you?" Gwen asked innocently, placing the monitor by his office phone.

"Sweetheart, you've been 'bothering' me for seven years. I wouldn't want you to stop now," he quipped.

She smiled and leaned over to give him a too brief kiss. "I missed you."

His heart leapt. *Nope, I will never get used to this.* "Sorry, I had some work to finish, but I was planning on heading up very soon."

"I figured, but I couldn't wait any longer to share my good news with you," she said with an infectious smile.

"Good news?" he asked, smiling too.

"Yes, I heard back from *The New York Times* Op-Ed department today. They agreed to give me a thousand words."

"That's wonderful!"

"It's not a paid gig, but it's certainly more credible and wider-reaching than a tabloid, which would have given me money for my story," Gwen gushed. "But it's not about that, since a piece like this could potentially allow me to be taken seriously as a writer again, while also setting the record straight. It's a win-win."

Taking her hands in his, Reade squeezed them in encouragement. "I agree. Sounds like the perfect opportunity. Congratulations!"

"Thank you. It's all due to your urging." She beamed at him. "I'm really excited. After it's published, I can start pounding on the doors of different editorial desks and looking for a position again, with my head held high."

"In New York?" he questioned.

"Well... yes, that's where most of the bigger publishing houses are headquartered." Pinning her bottom lip with her teeth, Gwen paused for a moment, then rushed forward. "New York, or another major metro area, and I can always see about trying to work remotely...maybe."

Gently, Reade lifted her chin and looked into her wary eyes. "I want you to go wherever will make you happy."

After a deep breath, Gwen whispered, "Being with you makes me happy."

"Then, I'll happily go wherever you find a position that you're excited about. If you want me to, that is."

Gwen released a breath that she wasn't aware she had been holding. "You will?" She flung herself onto Reade's lap. His leather office chair rocked back precariously in the process. But before her lips touched his, the implications of what he'd said sunk in. "But what about your firm?"

"I only moved back here because my mother was sick, so I could be near her. Then, after she passed, I stayed because of you," he said poignantly.

Gwen smiled with all the love she felt. "I stayed because you were here, too. It's one of the main reasons why I never moved to D.C."

"Then nothing is keeping us here, if we leave together," he said logically. "Our New York branch would more than welcome me to the team, as would any of our other offices around the world. That's a benefit of being a partner—job security. Plus, Danielle is more than capable of heading up this practice without me."

"But... Is there any family that you'd want to be near?" Gwen asked. "We've talked about your mother, but I don't remember you mentioning anyone else."

"No one I want to be around," Reade replied defensively.

Catching his suddenly harsh tone, Gwen stared at him. He was being evasive, but she wasn't sure why. "Is your father still alive?" she prompted. "I don't know anything about him."

"That makes two of us, and no, he died a few years ago."

"I'm sorry, Reade." She brought her hands up to his shoulders and gently massaged them.

"Don't be. I didn't even know he was my dad until my mom's deathbed confession. He was married to someone else, and my mom was one of his employees, and then came me. Apparently, he bought our house for us and occasionally gave her some money for child support, but he never even acknowledged me or my mother, and after he died, it was like we never happened. No mention in his will, not that I was expecting anything. Not even a note or an apology letter. We were just the other family he didn't want."

"That's terrible. I do remember Jesse saying how you grew up not knowing who your father was," Gwen recalled.

"Of course he told you, just like he told our entire high school. He always made it sound as if I was some discarded baby on a doorstep and my mom some trashy woman who couldn't remember who my father was," Reade said angrily.

"Ugh, what a prick!" Gwen said, outraged on his behalf. "Now that I think about it, he did seem to take pleasure in telling me about it."

"Of course he would, when—" Reade cut himself off midsentence.

"When, what?" Gwen demanded, cringing at the sharpness of her tone. She didn't mean to sound like a curious reporter, but Reade wasn't telling her the whole story—she could feel it in her gut.

"Nothing," he said, turning his head away from her.

Gwen squeezed her hands on his shoulders again in comfort. "Why didn't your mom tell you who your dad was sooner?"

"I suppose she didn't want me resenting him." Reade shrugged. "He lived here, in town, and she feared the gossip. I think she might have still been in love with him, and maybe wanted to protect him and keep his other family from knowing."

"He had other kids? You have brothers and sisters?" she asked excitedly.

"He had another son, a few months older than me," he said with another shrug.

"Have you two met?" she prodded.

Throwing her a hurt-filled glance, he answered gravely, "Yes. We were childhood friends."

Gwen gasped. "Oh, my God! Oh, my God... Jesse is your brother. Your half-brother." It wasn't a question, but Reade nodded, and her breath came out in a whoosh. "Holy shit!"

She reflexively scooted off his lap to stand, before returning immediately to hug him to her, knowing how difficult this must be for him. Suddenly, a new thought ran through her brain. "That makes Maddie your niece. You two really are family!"

"Yes, my niece," Reade said, hugging Gwen tighter, "goddaughter, and future stepdaughter."

Gwen's heart lurched at the last descriptor. It was far from a proposal, so she tried her best to keep her emotions under control. Breaking the tension, she teasingly asked, "You plan on marrying Jesse?"

"Ha ha, very funny." Reade playfully slapped her butt in reprimand.

"Does Jesse know?"

"That you and I are getting married?" he joked back.

Gwen couldn't control her gasp that time. He'd actually said it. Still far from a proposal, but his sincerity was definitely there. It had been a while since she had been single, but she knew men didn't throw around the M-word lightly. "You...you know what I meant. Does Jesse know you're his half-brother?"

. . .

Reade leaned back in his chair, wanting to continue teasing Gwen and not wanting to talk about Jesse. But he'd come this far, so he might as well tell her the whole thing. "Apparently, he found out back in high school, and wasn't happy about it. Ironically, we'd grown up feeling like brothers, even pretending that we were. I would sleep over at his estate and go along on trips with his mother and our father, all with neither of us knowing."

Gwen had started to pace during his explanation. "Then, why wouldn't he be happy to find out you were truly brothers? No, don't answer that," she said, putting up her hand in a halt motion. "I know, because he's selfish jerk and he feared a scandal."

"Yes, and I imagine he was angry at our dad for cheating on his mom. Jesse was always competitive. Even before he found out, he'd been envious that our dad would praise my grades but not his. Looking back, it explains why Jesse, Sr., took an interest in me at all. At the time, I thought he was just a friend's father being nice to me, but now I think that it was fatherly pride, even if he didn't want to acknowledge me that way."

"All of which helped to fuel Jesse's animosity toward you and his drive to succeed. This explains a lot about him," Gwen mused aloud.

"Well, I'm glad I could enlighten you, Dr. Freud," he sniped.

"No, don't get me wrong." Stopping her pacing, she returned to his side to place a kiss on his creased brow. Firmly cradling his face, she forced him to look directly into her loving eyes. "As a journalist, this was the missing piece to the story, what I've been trying to figure out about him from the beginning, and it all fits now. Finally. I could never understand his need to succeed as if something was chasing him. It also explains a lot about you and why you turned out so much better than he did. I know it might not seem like it, but you were better off not growing up in that mansion, with that cold father, ambivalent mother, and all the family expectations that went with it."

"I've come to that conclusion too," Reade admitted. "I know I'm making it all sound terrible, but my mother was wonderful, loving, and hardworking. I actually had a really happy childhood despite an absentee father. It's just hard not to be bitter sometimes."

"Of course, who wouldn't be? But unlike Jesse, you didn't let it dictate your life." Brushing her lips down to his temple, Gwen added, "I'm so proud of you."

Reade wrapped his arms around her and gathered her close, feeling lighter and stronger, having released the secret that had haunted him most of his life. It felt good to let it out, especially when he had Gwen in his arms to accept it all.

Abruptly pushing away, Gwen looked up at Reade with a new concern in her eyes. "You must have hated me for choosing Jesse over you, like your dad. No wonder why I'd catch you sometimes glancing at me with such anger and hurt in your eyes."

Smiling, Reade shook his head and pulled Gwen back into his arms. "No, those looks weren't aimed at you. At fate, perhaps, for putting the one woman I wanted with Jesse of all people. It seemed like further proof that he got all the lucky breaks, without even trying. The anger you saw, though, was likely sexual frustration, from you driving me crazy. Like you're doing right now," he said, at the end of his control. With one arm anchored around Gwen's waist, he slid his other hand down, over the curve of her butt, and boosted her up onto his desk.

"Now?" Gwen asked, with her mischievous smirk that he found sexy as all hell. She placed her palms on the desk's surface, arching her back and thrusting her breasts up in a delicious offering beneath his hungry gaze.

"Definitely now," Reade groaned looking at her, gently urging her to lie back fully on the desktop, his body moving between her legs. He trailed his mouth down the graceful column of her neck to her cleavage, but hesitated above her heaving chest. "Say it," he demanded.

"I love you," Gwen said simply and honestly.

"I love you, too. Always have and always will," Reade said huskily, gathering her back upright into his arms for a hungry kiss that he hoped communicated his promise.

Groaning, he moved his arms down her back to cup her ass, he desperately pulled her closer to his hard body. Papers and office supplies cascaded down to the floor, but Reade didn't care. The only thing he cared about was in his arms, driving him wild.

Grasping the hem of her top, Reade flipped it upwards, grunting when he discovered she wasn't wearing a bra. Gwen gulped, her nipples instantly stabbing up into the cool air of the office. Wasting no time, he palmed her full breasts. Gently massaging her stiff nipples with the pads of his thumbs, he coaxed a low moan from her throat.

Goddamn, he was hard.

Pulling her leggings and panties down to her ankles with more force than was needed, Reade followed the garments with his tongue, letting the stubble of his five-o-clock shadow lightly rasp against her creamy, smooth thighs.

With a wolfish smile, Reade licked his lips and positioned her back down on the desk's surface. Gathering her ankles, he placed them alongside her bare ass at the very edge of his desk so that her wet core was revealed further to him. Taking her in, Reade almost didn't want to move and ruin the vision before him.

Almost.

But if he didn't taste her soon, he might just have a heart

attack. The hurried beating in his chest matched the desperate pulsing of his cock, urging him to take her.

Gwen's sexy whimper got him moving again. Locking eyes on her, he slowly descended his mouth to savor his prize.

"I need to taste you," Reade said hoarsely as he roughly buried his face between her quivering thighs, eliciting an immediate gasp from Gwen.

Reade drew her clit into the warmth of his mouth and suckled it. Gwen bucked instinctually. With a muffled laugh, he palmed her ass, bringing her more firmly into contact with his hungry explorations as he greedily lapped at her folds, suctioning them repeatedly into his mouth.

"Please, Reade. I can't take much more," she begged.

Reade heard her breathy plea somewhere in the back of his lust-fogged mind. More than happy to oblige, he sucked harder and harder still, until her head fell back on a groan as she came violently and he licked up her release.

"Oh. My. God." Panting, Gwen let her legs fall numbly off his desk. "You better be joining me now," she demanded, reaching out her arms to him. "Better yet, time to cash in that rain check that you promised me, because I've always had this fantasy of barging in here. Placing my finger over your sexy lips to block any questions or protests. Then, getting down on my knees before you and sucking you off right here in your office."

That delicious scenario so matched his own fantasies that it took Reade a second to find his voice. "Fuck yes," he growled through clenched teeth, his nostrils flaring. "But baby, I won't last. I almost came at your words just now. I promise we'll do that and much, much more in the future. Right now, I just need to sink inside you."

"Then, what are you waiting for?" she asked, opening her legs and wiggling herself closer to him.

Unable to resist any longer, he freed himself from his pants and rubbed his steel-hard erection against her moist flesh, softly groaning from the delicious contact.

"Reade!" Gwen exclaimed, with more than a hint of annoyance in her voice. "For freak's sake, now!"

Well, hell. His girl was as greedy as he was, it seemed. "Yes, ma'am," he drawled with an arrogant smile, thrusting into her, the force of his entry scooting her up higher on his desk as he sheathed himself completely in her heat.

Bracing himself above her, Reade retreated back out completely. Gwen's aching sigh at the loss of him had him smiling, but when he plunged back inside her, he was no longer playing. The time for teasing was gone, and so was Reade's control. She felt too damn good.

His movements were frantic as he ground hard against her, applying pressure to her sensitized clit with each undulation.

Gwen arched her back again, molding herself even closer to where their bodies were joined, wrapping her legs around his hips. *Fuck*, she was clawing at his back like a wild woman, and he savored every needy touch.

"Yes," she cried out, writhing beneath him, her breathing labored. On a long, lusty groan, her second orgasm burst forth, her legs trembling around him as she came.

The feel of Gwen's release quickened his, and after a few glorious strokes he joined her, finding his own bliss.

It took all of Reade's remaining strength to keep from collapsing on top of her and to shake off the tunnel vision enveloping him. Lifting her into his arms, he fell back onto his leather chair. Settling Gwen on his lap, he clutched her close to his chest as their breathing eventually returned to normal.

"I thought I had a vivid imagination where you were concerned," Reade heaved, lightly stroking Gwen's naked back. "But that just topped my fantasies."

"Mine, too," she said with a lusty sigh. "But I still have plenty of more fantasies starring you to *brief* you on counselor."

Reade chuckled, feeling like the luckiest bastard in the world. "Well, sweetheart, I am happy to *cross examine* your fantasies further, but I warn you, I'm nothing if not thorough."

It was her turn to laugh. "Then clear your afternoon tomorrow, as I believe I have a rain check to redeem. Right here."

Nodding his head, Reade agreed, "Tomorrow," his voice husky and serious. "And the rest of my life—I'm yours."

14

"*I* really appreciate you taking the time to meet with me," Gwen said while scanning Danielle Dixon's stoic office.

Not one personal photo or knickknack adorned the professional space. It was just as polished as Gwen had expected, but the councilor's bare feet and cast-aside Louboutin heels came as a surprise. Instead of the composed knockout that she'd only had glimpses of previously, this version of Danielle seemed more approachable, seated at her desk chair with her legs tucked up underneath her.

"Of course," the auburn beauty said with a smile that was both sympathetic and genuine.

Releasing her tight shoulders, Gwen sank into the open chair in front of the large mahogany desk.

"First of all, I'm so sorry," Danielle said with a direct stare that seemed to see right into Gwen's soul. Or maybe she was being hopeful? It had been so long since she'd had another woman to talk openly with.

With a nervous laugh, Gwen shook her head. "Why? You didn't take all my money and leave me for a younger woman."

Danielle guffawed, and in that instant Gwen knew they shared a real connection beyond her ex. "This is true," Danielle huffed. "But we scorned Jesse's girls have to stick together, after all."

No sooner had Danielle uttered those words than her manicured hand rose to cover her surprised expression. "I'm so sorry," she muttered behind her fingers. "I don't mean to make light of your situation. Really! It's just that I feel a bond with you, having been somewhat in your shoes before. Jesse might have left this whole damn town shocked, but not me. Well, not anymore, at least."

Like a bobble head doll, Gwen nodded eagerly, wanting to hear more even as she let Danielle's words sink in. Some of the weight of Jesse's betrayal lifted off Gwen's shoulders. She wasn't the only one duped by the guy. "I'm sorry I'm not the only one he used," she said with a sigh. "I know you two dated in high school, but I wasn't aware of any bad blood."

"Well, I'd like to think that I've done my best to put it behind me."

Gwen waited for Danielle to continue, but she seemed lost in her own memories. The silence stretched. Probably only a few seconds, but it felt like the longest pause ever. "Oh, please don't stop there!"

Danielle released a silent chuckle and nodded. "I've known him since Kindergarten... and Reade, too," Danielle continued. "Even as a kid, Jesse was always so damn perfect, at least in front of others. To the point that no one even questioned it. I know I didn't. He ran every club, was the head of every activity, and so charming."

Gwen nodded, easily picturing him as an overachieving kid. "What happened to change that?" she prodded, knowing all too well where the story was likely headed.

"I was a tomboy, you see," she added with a laugh at Gwen's confusion. "That's right, you came to Dodge after my makeover." She tilted her head toward the discarded heels by the door. "My feet still aren't used to the change either, but I swear, I was an awkward teenager raised by my dad and brothers. Even my best friend, Hunter, was a jock. The only girlfriends I had were there just so they could try and catch Hunter's eye. Then came senior year and suddenly Jesse Clark started paying attention to me. All the other girls were so jealous and thought I was just the luckiest ever to be friends with Hunter and have Jesse taking me to prom." Danielle trailed off with a sigh. "I didn't even want to be his girlfriend, really, but I suddenly felt seen. He just... He said and did everything a lonely girl could ever want, and I blindly did everything he asked."

"Wait, time out," Gwen interrupted, holding up her hands in surrender. "Are you mimicking me? Because this sounds like you're practically telling my story right now. Well, I wasn't a tomboy, but I was lonely and grieving. I felt special to have his attention."

"I thought that might be the case." Reaching over the nameplate on her desk, Danielle held out her hands to Gwen in comfort and solidarity. Gwen readily took hold, glad to be understood.

"But you guys were kids, what was the end game?" Gwen asked.

Danielle shrugged her shoulders. "I think I was an easy target then, someone he could manipulate. I did his homework, I let him cheat off my tests, and even defended him to Hunter, when he accused Jesse of planting weed in his locker. Basically, teen drama at its finest. Minus the happy John Hughes ending."

"If Jesse had something to gain from Hunter's failing, then I have no doubt he was behind it."

"Oh he had a lot to gain. Because of the school's drug policy, Hunter was thrown off the football team, and Jesse took over as quarterback, earning the eye of the college scouts. Despite not having his back, Hunter still warned me against going to prom with Jesse. Of course I did, though.

"I'm afraid to ask...was prom was fun at least?"

"No, but is prom ever fun for anyone?" Danielle asked. "Except for Jesse, that is. He was named prom king. It was that night that I started to see the real side of him. He was picking fights with Hunter and Reade for no reason. And when I said I had to be home by midnight, he raved about his reputation and how I was expected to go to his family's cabin with him. I didn't go, but he told everyone I did and more."

"I'm sorry," Gwen marveled.

"Honestly, I really didn't care what everyone thought. The worst part was losing my real best friend. Who, get this, I'm actually about to see for the first time in thirteen years, and I'm kinda freakin' out, but that's a whole other story."

"That's exciting at least! Maybe the end credits haven't played yet for your Hughes film."

"You're funny," Danielle said, shaking her head. "No, he's finally coming back home to take over his dad's business, and I'm the family attorney who will be managing the transition. I'm not sure he even knows that part yet. Anyway, the past is in the past. I might have been powerless then, but I've got the law behind me this time. Let's get you unmarried from that professional shithead ASAP, shall we?"

"Yes, please!" Gwen practically cheered. Where the hell was a marching band when she needed one?

"I have to warn you, it's going to be a little complicated, but not impossible."

Gwen couldn't help but groan. Nothing was easy, was it? "That doesn't sound good."

"We can't simply serve the fucker with divorce papers like in a normal divorce, since we have no idea where he is. So, I suggest we file on the grounds of abandonment. However, in

Texas abandonment typically requires desertion of a spouse for at least one year."

"A whole year?" Gwen asked, unable to prevent her sullen tone.

"No." Danielle gripped her hand once again in reassurance. "I'm hoping to prove the intention of abandonment. Thanks to the press, Jesse's hasty departure with another woman has been well documented and will hopefully function as evidence."

Who would have thought Gwen would one day be thankful for the recent invasion of her privacy?

"Not to mention that he is no longer supporting you or his daughter financially," Danielle said, matter-of-factly. "I'm hoping to get Judge Gonzalez to hear the case, since she is new to the area and will likely be more sympathetic to your situation, without preconceived notions about the great Clark family. Fingers crossed."

"Oh, I'm crossing more than that," Gwen said, crossing her arms and legs in demonstration. "Thank you so much, I feel better knowing I have you in my corner."

"My pleasure. Believe me, I'm going to enjoy this. Loopholes and all. Besides, I'm not the only one in your corner," Danielle added suggestively. "Reade has assured me he'll call on all his contacts if needed. He seems pretty motivated to get you free from Jesse as well."

Tingly heat rose to Gwen's cheeks, and Danielle's teasing laughter confirmed she was blushing.

"Alright, I'll leave that line of questioning for one night over drinks, just us girls, how does that sound?" Danielle got up from her chair and walked toward her.

"Like I'm thirsty already."

"Great answer," Danielle said, leading Gwen to the door. "I'll get things rolling, and you'll be hearing from me shortly about next steps *and* happy hour."

Gwen stilled before walking through the door. "Um, Danielle?

"Yes?"

"I know, I'm not the best person to give out love advice, but don't make the same mistakes I did. My life would have been very different if I'd had the courage to tell Reade how I felt earlier. Took a chance."

"I... It's too late. Too much water under the bridge."

"It's never too late. It took me seven years, but I'm hoping to finally have my happily ever after. You deserve one too, Danielle. With or without Hunter."

15

*G*wen beamed up at the man occupying her thoughts as they strolled home together on a particularly hot afternoon the following week. *Speaking of hot...* She had always thought that she'd enjoyed sex before, but at the same time, she'd survived well enough without it over the years. Making love with Reade, though, was in a different league altogether. Apparently, she had been stuck in the amateur circuit and was now in the hands of a pro.

Last night, during another mind-blowing escapade in bed together, Reade had once again demonstrated his passion, leisurely taking his time caressing and pleasing her like never before. Shaking her head at the memory, Gwen still couldn't believe that she had actually begged, whimpered, and pleaded for him to stop gloriously tormenting her and to help her find the release that he kept deliciously prolonging.

"Oh honey, I've only just begun." Reade's heated reply and languid chuckle still gave her goosebumps. "You have no idea all the things that I want to do to you, with you, for you. Go ahead and suffer."

If she hadn't already been lying down, entangled in his

arms, surely she would have melted from the heat of his erotic promise. Fortunately, he didn't make her wait much longer, roughly whispering some of the things he had planned for them as he stroked her, bringing her to a blinding orgasm.

Beyond the amazing sexual compatibility that left her with very little sleep each night, simply being together as a couple was magical. To openly and eagerly greet him when he came home. To talk in detail about their days. To have a friend and lover in one... Well, it felt like she had been handed the relationship that she'd always dreamt of. Yet, technically she was still married to someone else.

She only hoped the divorce would go through as smoothly and quickly as Danielle anticipated. Then, she would finally be free. Though really, Gwen felt free already, with or without a piece of paper to make it legal. Free of Jesse's control, free to love and be loved in return, free to just *be*, and it felt wonderful. Humming to herself, she walked up the steps to the apartment, holding Reade's hand and swinging their arms like two smitten teenagers.

And why not? It was a beautiful Sunday, and they had just spent an idyllic morning at the park watching Maddie and her team play. After, Maddie left with her friend Hannah to go to the team pizza party, celebrating the end of their softball season. Gwen was looking forward to some alone time with Reade in the short hours before Hannah's mom dropped Maddie off.

What was waiting for them at the top of the flight of stairs brought them both to a dead stop.

Jesse Clark stood on the landing with his arms and legs crossed, one shoulder leaning against the doorframe with a smug smirk on his face. And he did not seem the least bit surprised to see them together.

She immediately dropped her hold on Reade's hand.

"Jesse!" Gwen exclaimed, too stunned to think of anything else to say. What the heck was he doing here? How? Why?

"Darlin', I've missed you," Jesse drawled thickly, pulling Gwen forward into his arms and kissing her square on the mouth.

Stunned, Gwen hesitated a second before snapping out of her frozen state and pushing out of Jesse's embrace. How could he have the audacity to act like nothing had happened? And how did he look perfectly composed, like he'd just stepped out of a photoshoot and not the least bit like a harassed criminal on the run?

Staring at the American flag pin on the lapel of his blazer, Gwen finally found her voice. "What are you doing here?"

He gave her a sardonic look and flicked an irritated gaze toward Reade for the briefest of seconds. "*Me?*"

When he stepped closer, Gwen desperately held her arms out to keep him at bay. The roll of his eyes expressed exactly what he thought of her barricade.

"I'm here to see my wife and child, of course. I must say, I was more than a little annoyed to return and find out that my family has been shacking up here, with Reade of all people." Jesse glared over Gwen's shoulder at Reade who loomed protectively next to her. "But I guess I'm not surprised."

"*You* are annoyed?" Gwen gasped, flabbergasted at his audacity. Her initial shock at seeing him now turning to outrage.

"If I was able to discover your whereabouts this easily, the press could, too, and they would get the wrong idea. Imagine what that would look like?" Jesse responded with a tone of disgust.

"Oh, I can imagine exactly what it would look like to the press... How the stories would go. In fact, I don't have to imagine it. I've lived it with everything they printed about you and April," Gwen shot back.

With that, she pushed past him, flung open the door, and marched inside Reade's apartment, not looking back to see if either of the men followed her. She needed to move. The outside hallway had felt like it was closing in on her, but that was probably only Jesse's menacing presence making her want to run. Not able to keep still, she started to pace.

"I forgot how cute you are when you're angry," Jesse said from behind her, too close for comfort. "Sorry about that, dear, but the entanglement with April was unavoidable. I never meant for that to become public. You know I've shielded us from any scandals in the past. It was all her idea, and it worked out nicely, don't you agree?"

"What are you talking about?" Gwen asked incredulously, not stopping her restless pacing or even bothering to look at him. She felt as if an avalanche was getting ready to crash down on her again, and her steady movements were the only thing keeping the imminent blow at bay. To think, she had been blissfully happy only moments before. The unfairness of it all made her want to cry.

While Gwen was on the verge of tears, Reade's gaze was trained on Jesse, and his expression was murderous.

"It was meaningless, believe me. I'm not stupid enough to fall for my intern," Jesse said calmly.

Meaningless? Bastard!

He reached out and put a firm hand on her shoulder, which felt like a vise, and Gwen immediately jerked free. "Grab me again and I'll call the police," she seethed.

"Go ahead," he said, not seeming the least bit phased, "but will you stop your fidgeting, at least? You know I hate it when you do that."

Gwen stopped, not because he'd ordered her to, but because Jesse seemed totally unconcerned about her threat to call the authorities. Why? He was on the run, after all. Was he merely calling her bluff, or did he really not care? What did he know that she didn't? All the unanswered questions gave her pause. Once again, it felt like Jesse was a few steps ahead of her on the chessboard of life. She stood there, woodenly frozen like a pawn.

"Thank you," Jesse said, with a curt nod of his head once she came to a stop. "I had ended it with April months ago, but she was cleverer than most and ambitious, too. She'd discovered that I was paying for a few political favors by skimming a little off the top of the Foundation's bank account. No one would have ever noticed, since I'd had it arranged to look like it was simply a payment to one of the gala vendors. However, April threatened to go public with both our brief affair and the missing funds if I didn't go along with her plan to take it all and run away with her. Given those two options, I didn't have much choice but to play along for a bit, naturally. In the end, though, it was April who diverted the money to an offshore account in her name, which is what I've explained to the FBI."

"You've talked with the FBI?" Gwen asked skeptically, not wanting to even touch the rest of his woe-is-me confession that he had no choice but to play along. He expected her to believe that the whole mess—the affair, the embezzlement—was all April's fault? *Puh-lease.* He might have charmed the FBI with that scenario, but she wasn't buying it.

"Doesn't this musty attic have a TV?" Jesse asked, giving Reade's spacious apartment a glance of disgust. "Haven't you heard the good news? I have been cleared of all charges."

"Just like that?" Reade's deep voice interrupted from behind them, along with a forceful snap of his fingers.

"No, not just like that," Jesse mocked, snapping as well. "A little quid pro quo was needed. It's all just politics, after all," he lectured, as he had often done during their marriage. "I provided them with the account numbers, which linked back to April only, along with some titillating information about several politicians that will keep them busily working on new cases for quite some time. Turn on the news. I'm being touted as a hero for revealing the entire scheme and working with the FBI in their ongoing investigations of governmental misconduct. It looks as if it was my plan all along to unearth capital corruptions. They're calling it a sting operation, can you believe that? I have an interview scheduled tomorrow with *Top Line* to continue spinning everything in my favor. We leave for Los Angeles in an hour."

"We?" Gwen and Reade asked almost simultaneously.

"Of course, we need to be a united front," Jesse said, grasping Gwen's hands in his, effectively pulling her further away from Reade. "I need my beautiful family by my side, with my courageous wife telling everyone how she doubted the accusations from the beginning, but never doubted our love."

"*Hmph*, so you want me to lie." It was a statement, not a question, and Gwen didn't bother waiting for a response. Pulling her hands away, she asked, "What about our money?"

"Well, I had to give that to April to buy her off, now that she has to live in exile in South America and everything." Jesse shrugged dismissively. "But don't worry, I'm on my way to earning a lot more. It's like I always say, you can't buy publicity like this."

"Or in your case, steal," Reade mumbled.

"Do you mind?" Jesse spat, throwing Reade a vicious look. "I would like to speak with *my* wife alone. This doesn't concern you."

Gwen interrupted before Reade could respond to that loaded remark. "You are delusional if you think I would take you back, Jesse, not after what I just went through. I'm finally getting off the merry-go-round, thank you. I've filed for divorce."

"What about Madilyn?" Jesse asked smugly.

"What about her?" she retorted.

"I'm her father," he stated, using the affable voice that he typically reserved for the camera.

"Some father. I bet you wouldn't know her birthday without your staff around to remind you. Do you know that she hasn't asked for you once since you've been gone? Actually, she's happier than ever, and so am I for that matter," she shot back.

"Be smart, Gwen," Jesse said coldly, through gritted teeth. "If you try to leave me, I'll make sure you never see her again. I know judges from here to the Capitol. I'll get full custody. Believe me, a working single dad would poll just as well, if not better, than the tiresome happy family picture."

His threat, issued with such calm and intent, stopped Gwen in her tracks and drained the color from her face. Damn if he didn't smile at her distress too, knowing that he had her right where he wanted her. All over again.

"Not with me as her lawyer," Reade said, gently pulling Gwen close to his side, offering her comfort and support. "Now, it's your turn to be smart, *brother*. You wouldn't want Gwen to share every dirty little secret that she knows about you in her tell-all magazine piece would you?"

Jesse had been rolling his eyes until he heard Reade say "brother." His lips curled into a sneer. "Don't ever call me that!" he yelled, before seeming to process the rest of Reade's words. "What piece? What is he talking about?" he demanded, turning back to Gwen.

Catching on, Gwen smiled, enjoying the feeling of having something to hold over Jesse, for once. "Several outlets offered me money for an interview about your infidelity and the theft, but, naturally, I declined them all."

"That's my girl," Jesse said, his initial sneer gradually turning back to a superior-looking expression. "I was keeping up on the news while I was away, and I admired that you were not speaking to those vultures without me. That's why we are such a good team."

Forget delusional, he's psychotic. She was already savoring the letdown she was about to deliver. "However," she said, then paused in order to drag the moment out more. "Reade encouraged me to write my own story. I pitched the idea of an op-ed piece to the *New York Times*, and they gave me a thousand words and carte blanche to write whatever I want about our so-called marriage and the scandal. Maybe I should add some pertinent family details of yours, for extra color?"

"You... You wouldn't dare."

"I would, and I *will*."

Jesse's face contorted in anger. So changed were his features that no one would be able to recognize him as the smooth-talking boy next door that he usually projected. "I'd sue you for slander!"

"It would be the truth, which you know is damning enough," Gwen pointed out.

"He said, she said," Jesse mocked, crossing his arms over his chest in an effort to appear relaxed. He was anything but; Gwen knew him well enough to know that.

Smiling, she went in for the kill. "You know as well as I do, once a defamatory seed is planted in the media, it will always be in the minds of the people, creating doubt, even if you were somehow able to prove what I write is wrong. You might be able to survive the current scandal, but another? I think not."

Reade added fuel to Gwen's fire. "As a lawyer, I would also like to point out that claiming libel or slander is a hard case to win, and usually brings out more dirty laundry and only garners further unwanted attention in the process."

"Shut the hell up, Walker!" Jesse hissed, his nice-guy façade completely gone now. He turned on Gwen. "You're nothing without me," he sputtered.

"You're wrong," she said serenely, with a confident smile. "I'll finally be someone again without you. No longer playing second fiddle to your career or your blind ambitions. I am going to get back the person I used to be."

Boy, did that feel great to say. She'd always known it, so it was about time she did something about it. But of course, not at the expense of her daughter. "Then again, if you agree to an amicable split and give me sole custody, I'll forget about writing the piece altogether. Heck, I'll even sign a confidentiality agreement stating I'll never share anything about our farce of a marriage."

"That is what it was, you know, a farce," Jesse bit back, trying to bait her further, not being able to stand losing, especially to her. "I never loved you. I only started seeing you for the story that you were writing and then married you for the free press that our relationship was garnering. It was one of the smartest political moves of my career." Turning to look at Reade, he added with an evil smirk, "Torturing you was just a bonus."

"Don't you have a plane to catch?" Reade replied drolly.

Gwen could tell by his tense frame that Reade was doing his best to keep his anger in check and control the urge to forcefully remove Jesse from the apartment and from their lives, once and for all.

Sauntering toward the door, Jesse bitterly spewed, "I guess you never did mind my castaways, little brother. It's like how the saying goes: one man's trash, is another man's treasure.'"

Jesse's vicious cackle faded quickly when Reade's fist connected with his mouth, leaving Jesse reeling. Gwen took hasty advantage of his confused state to shove Jesse out the door, then delighted in slamming it shut behind him with a sigh of relief. *Boy, did that feel great!*

Reade breathed his own sigh of relief. "That felt great," he said, echoing her thoughts with a broad smile.

∼

Reade took even greater pleasure in seeing Jesse's swollen lip during his primetime interview the following evening. As he sat, snuggled on the couch with Gwen, he watched Jesse lie to the television host while Maddie slept in the den. Reade was already planning on converting the room into a proper children's bedroom, one fit for a princess. *A baseball princess*, he amended, thinking of her two current passions.

And if Gwen found a job opportunity in New York or another city, they'd look for a place there. It didn't matter where they ended up, as long as they all lived there together, because if Reade had learned anything, it was that Gwen and Maddie were his anchors. He was only a shell of a person without them. Now, with them by his side, his life was full of possibilities again.

Still, it was annoying seeing Jesse successfully slime his way out of trouble and into favor again, like an alley cat, always landing on his feet. But soon, Jesse would be just another politician on television, and thankfully no longer in their lives. Reade would make sure of that, working with Danielle to serve Jesse with divorce papers as soon as possible and finally making Gwen and Maddie *his* girls. His family.

Life is good, Reade thought, as he pulled back Gwen's golden locks and nuzzled the spot below her ear. Her happy giggle tickled his heart.

Lady Luck must like me after all. Even if she took the roundabout way to deliver her prize.

With a satisfied smile, Reade asked, "Gwen, do you believe in love at first sight?"

The End

BOOK CLUB QUESTIONS

- What was your initial reaction to the book? Did it hook you immediately, or take some time to get into?
- Was it weak of Gwen to have stayed in her sham marriage to Jesse? In what ways was it strong?
- How do Gwen and Reade grow throughout the course of the story?
- What was your favorite scene? Why did it stand out?
- Do you think Jesse will ever receive his due for his duplicities? Was losing Gwen enough?
- What do you think of the book's title? How does it relate to the plot?

ACKNOWLEDGMENTS

A huge thank you to my friend and editor Rebecca Andersen for going on this journey with me.

To author Farrah Rochon for showing me that it was possible.

And to the Southwest Florida Romance Writers Association.

MINE TO FIVE

'TIS THE SEASON FOR AN OFFICE ROMANCE

CHAPTER ONE

Nothing good can come from another woman answering your guy's cell phone.

Melanie Thomas came to this epiphany the moment she heard the unfamiliar female voice on the other end of the phone line. She did a double take to make sure she'd selected the correct name from her contact list, but sure enough, clear as day, it read Joe. *Her* Joe.

He didn't have a sister either and his mother had passed away. That left three likely possibilities. None were pleasant, and all spelled doom for her relationship.

Possibility number one, would go something like, "Hello this is Mrs. Kinnear, please stop calling my husband, you tramp!"

Melanie dismissed the idea as quickly as it surfaced. After almost two years of dating, surely she would have ferreted out a wife by now, right?

Possibility number two, the mystery woman was a concerned police officer, medic or bystander who would solemnly say, "I am so sorry to be the one to inform you, but there has been a terrible accident. His last request is to see your beautiful face again. Please hurry!"

She really shouldn't hope for this scenario, but a horrible, selfish part of her preferred it to the last option.

No, sadly, possibility number three was the most probable reason for why another woman was answering her boyfriend's phone at night. Even her shocked mind registered this option was more like probability number one. Her boyfriend was having an affair, plain and simple, or rather pain and simple.

"Hello?" the feminine voice repeated after Melanie had failed to get her tongue-tied mouth to answer the first time.

From her voice alone Melanie could tell the other woman had to be sexy. Her predatory purr dripped of confidence laced with a tinge of malice.

Melanie cringed, but she managed to ask over the peach-sized pit lodged in her throat, "Is Joe Kinnear there?" Sucking in her breath, she braced for the unknown woman's answer.

"Of course, let me wake him up," taunted the sultry, young voice.

Wake him up? She hunched forward from the invisible sucker punch. *Yup, definitely scenario three. He's cheating!*

Staring at the blue glow from her phone, she noticed the call time count. Twenty seconds, that was how long it took to unravel a relationship of twenty months. Cradling the phone in the crook of her neck, Melanie covered her other ear with her palm and tried to block out the noise of the busy club as she waited.

To think, moments earlier she had been eager for the night ahead, especially since Joe had something important to discuss with her. That, paired with the fact that she was celebrating the start of a new job at a major advertising firm tomorrow—a job that would make her career—had Melanie elated as she'd walked through the steel doors of the trendy Manhattan nightclub Surge. Everything in her life had seemed to be aligning for her. The tide had finally been turning, and Melanie was more than ready to have it roll her way. It had all been going as planned, except now it wasn't.

~

Coming Soon!

ALSO BY TARA SEPTEMBER

It Might Be You (Short Story)

ABOUT THE AUTHOR

Blogger and former PR executive, Tara holds a Master's degree in journalism and communications from NYU. For over a decade, she has penned a popular lifestyle, travel and parenting blog at TaraMetBlog.com.

An avid romance reader, she has been daydreaming about being a romance author since high school. Dozens of bad dates and adventures later, she still finds it impossible that she met her husband on a New York City subway. Now they live in sunny Southwest Florida with identical twin boys and four cats underfoot. When the kids are asleep and the cats are not lying on her keyboard, she's finally writing the happily ever after tales she's been dreaming about. www.TaraSeptember.com

facebook.com/taraseptemberauthor

twitter.com/taraseptember

instagram.com/taraseptemberauthor

Made in the
USA
Lexington, KY